KEN ROBBINS

I would like to thank my wife Joanne and son Tim for their support and patience while I spent countless hours writing and revising over the last eighteen months.

Contents

CHAPTER 1

THE GARAGE

The last ball rocketed off the red side of Mark Linderman's paddle, and he switched off the power strip. From the side door of the frosty two car garage, he dashed inside the house, and directly into the kitchen.

"Hi Mom."

"Good morning."

Mark bellied up to the counter, and between scoops of his honey drizzled oatmeal, he scanned his tablet for table tennis news. A red bulletin flashed on Scott Kobara's home page.

My Magnificent Table Tennis Cruise is sold out as of March 1st. I apologize to those who were unable to obtain a reservation.

Mark opened the *cruise tab* and dove into details. "Hey, check this out. Some of the best players in the world are going to be on a ship!"

Table Tennis Themed Mediterranean Cruise. Restricted to 24 players rated 2500 and above. One significant other is allowed. Players under 18 must be accompanied by at least one parent or guardian. The

Ping of the Seas will depart June 8th from Miami, Florida, and return July 14th. European players will board from Lisbon, Portugal June 17th, and return there July 7th. The ports of call will be Valletta, Corfu, and Durres.

"It looks right up your alley, and out of our price range. How about we just paint ocean murals on the garage walls?"

"Very funny, but when I'm eighteen."

"That's a lot of odd jobs to do in two years, and I don't think it's approved for financial aid. Can you help me scrape the ice off again this morning? I'm going in early to help Mrs. Moss make posters for the library."

Mark finished the car windows and Candice Linderman turned from the driveway. Mark waved and darted right back into the garage. The ceiling lights flickered as he switched on the lone space heater under the ping pong table. The glowing coils did little to stave off the northern Montana cold, but Mark was used to practicing in hot and cold extremes.

Atop a wooden stool facing him, sat a robot, a table tennis robot that is. One that spews out multiple balls in all directions with the cadence of a popcorn popper. The robot didn't rip Mark for his passion, like a handful of students. It just fired away, relentlessly. The town of Chinook had less than two thousand people, and Knoll Edge High School needed all the students it could get to fill the sports teams. Kids were bused in from the surrounding towns, but the rosters were always hurting. Had he stepped up to the plate, no one would have cared that he loved table tennis so much. So the more pressure Mark got to play, the more he retreated and pounded the little white balls. With no worthy competition nearby, and not one sanctioned club within hundreds of miles, the garage remained his world.

Donning a camo t-shirt and sweats, Mark had a special ops look today. He switched on his electro-mechanical rival, and crouched, ready to return fire. His newest multi-ball bot groaned as it came up to speed, and the onslaught was upon him. He careened from side to side, launching back rockets with lightning reflexes, backhand and forehand. Warm blasts of breath darted out from him in dragon-like fashion. This guerilla training segment took less than three minutes for him to smack the two hundred plus balls.

Mark created games within the game; skill-sharpening drills which kept his practice sessions fresh, day after day. He developed scores of programs which resided within the robot's software. Dime-sized stickers served as targets for his precision shot making. *Acupuncture on the run*, he called it.

The last shots of his mid-day session slapped into a king-sized blue sheet, the first phase of his rudimentary collection system. In bucket brigade fashion, the balls followed each other down a cardboard gutter into the terminus, a blue laundry basket. Over and over he would dump the balls from the basket into the robot's hopper. Before exiting, Mark recorded his drills in his log, along with the thirty-nine degree garage temperature. Back inside, with a peanut butter sandwich in his left hand, he again tapped his tablet for articles on the cruise.

Exotic Table Tennis themed cruise quickly sells out, and entirely to Europeans.

The slamming of a car door announced Mark's father was home surprisingly early from work. Immediately upon entering the front door, his rant began.

"Having to park outside is giving my truck premature rust, and it's a royal pain scraping the ice off the windshield every morning. How about taking up a real sport?"

Mark's setup did monopolize the garage, but his dad couldn't have any issues with the cleanliness of it. Dirt and dust were the biggest enemies of the robots, so Mark maintained a surgical type of environment, mopping the floor, and wiping down the table each night. Once a week, all four hundred practice balls would be immersed and washed.

The friction in the house temporarily quelled Mark's interest in the article, so he left his tablet on the counter, and marched back out to his refuge. Candice walked in the front door and was immediately accosted.

"Can't you do something to get him to leave the garage? How about baseball? He's got great hand-eye coordination. My God, he's going to be a junior next year."

"He's happy in his world, and I can't go back on my promise."

"That was eight years ago we put the ping pong table in there."

"Yep, and he's gotten straight A's ever since."

"I never thought I'd like to see my son's grades fall. I forgot something at the hardware store. I'll be right back."

Candice picked up the phone and called her sister Kathy in Naples.

"Hey what's up?"

"The usual tension around here, but it seems to be worse with Mark this winter. Carl is digging at him more, especially since this cold seems to be lingering. There's two more years before Mark heads off to college. I don't know if I can take it."

"Why doesn't Mark come down here for a couple months this summer? I know of two table tennis clubs in the area, the ocean's not far, and of course I've got the pool and the dog. Mark can meet some live players and blow off some steam. It'll help everyone."

"Are you sure?"

"I know Carl's not crazy about me, but it's worth a try. I'll be around a lot. I do most of my work out of my house, except when I have to meet clients. Make a nice meal, and then pop the question."

"You're wonderful."

Steam rose as the family dissected their baked potatoes. Carl stabbed a pork chop from the center plate, and Candice mentally rehearsed her approach. As usual, Mark scoffed down his meal and ducked back into the garage.

"Kathy offered to have Mark stay with her in Naples this summer."

"You know how I feel about her. She got you busted once, and almost killed another time."

"That was in our early twenties. She's done with the whitewater and mountains. There's none around there anyway. She's had the same job for ten years."

"Elopement planner. Give me a break."

"She supports herself, and has done a lot of work on her house. Mark can play pong in the clubs there, with real people."

"It might not be the worst for him, as long as she behaves herself."

Candice zipped through the dishes, and exited out the side door into to the garage. Mark fumbled for his remote, and the robot's motor wound down, feebly spitting out the last ball.

"What's up mom?"

"You can take as long as you want to think about this, but I just wanted to tell you that your aunt offered for you to stay with her this summer. She said there's a couple clubs in the area."

"Wow, awesome. Dad's okay with it?"

"It's all good. We've got plenty of time to work out the details."

"Thanks mom."

Mark returned to the house, grabbed his tablet, and dove into the Naples' club's websites.

CHAPTER 2

THE SHIP

A golf cart careened up the long asphalt dock in the shipyards of Port Everglades. Scott Kobara rode alongside his project supervisor, and glanced upwards at the aging cruise ship. Above him, in fresh white paint, *The Ping of the Seas* graced the weathered hull. Seconds later, the cart screeched to a stop, and the two men walked past the guard and up the gangway.

"They were thinking about retiring her before you stepped in Mr. Kobara. We're moving right along, and I think she should be ready by June."

As the pair entered a bright and expansive area, the supervisor continued.

"You'd never know this used to be a casino. Half of the high-tech panes are in, and the floor is almost finished. Looking at the plans, those sixteen X's are exactly where you indicated the ping pong tables will go. As soon as we get them, we will anchor them down."

"That's all I needed," said Scott. "The cab is still waiting for me in the parking lot, and I need to get back to New York."

When they reached the lot, Scott climbed into the cab and the driver immediately asked, "Airport?"

"No. Take me into Miami, the thirty three hundred block of University."

Only a handful of cars sat in the parking lot of the light blue warehouse-like building. It was early afternoon on this Monday, and inside, a sweet metronome-like sound resonated throughout the facility. Scott walked in, and as if he had pressed the mute button, silence befell the building. Only two tables were in use, and all four players stared at the entrance.

"Scotty! What the heck brings you down here?" asked Sal, the owner. "Usually you're off playing in some foreign country."

"Well I've got time for a couple games. You know, I aim to play every day."

"Oh, now I know. You've got that cruise departing from here. We've got a few rich players who could afford it, but they don't have the rating."

"Yeah." Said Scott. "My game isn't worthy of being on board either, but since I'm hosting it, I get to play. You know those elite players, they don't want to play the lesser folk."

"But I see you've still got plenty of game. A 1500 rating isn't bad for a guy approaching seventy."

"Sixty-seven, don't rush it. Let's play when you're done over there."

"We're just practicing. Come on over."

From a pocket of his laptop case, Scott pulled out his paddle and dusted off Sal in three straight games.

"I'm out of here. It's back to Hawthorne."

"Thanks for the beating, and good luck with your cruise."

Scott was again whisked away in the waiting cab, and narrowly made his flight to LaGuardia.

Once inside his office at his impressive table tennis center, Scott picked up the Post-Times.

Scott Kobara, the wealthy and retired sound engineer has built and retrofitted concert halls around the world. The table tennis club owning fanatic has also taken his ping pong game around the globe, playing in some twenty five different countries. Some say the sixty-seven year old has gotten more eccentric, and turned away from his dreams to develop an American Champion.

He is chartering and retrofitting an aging cruise ship for a Mediterranean bound table tennis themed cruise. The exorbitant price, along with skepticism about play on the rough Atlantic, has deterred American players. Twenty four elite European players and their significant others though, have grabbed all the spots. The shorter cruise, stronger Euro, and extended vacations, have made the package relatively attractive for them. Kobara is expected to take a financial bath on the extravaganza.

Scott called in Skip, his facility manager, playing partner, and traveling companion.

"So what's the story on the tables?" asked Scott.

"The holdup is the legs, the sixty-four custom floor anchors and the locking feet. The retrofitters went with a small fabrication company because the big ones scoffed at the small quantity. It sounds like there's a delay in getting materials. It's going to be close to the wire."

"Yes, you don't have to tell me," Scott barked. "They would have been ready if I had chosen the imported parts. I want American materials, American made, and an American champion, contrary to that newspaper. We'll really look like fools if these aren't done in time. I'll chain the tables to the floor myself if I have to. Eccentric, they say. That's their derogatory word for creative. If I want to run an empty ship across the Atlantic, and lose my shirt on the cruise, that's my business."

"I saw that, but didn't want to bring it up," said Skip. "You knew there probably wouldn't be any Americans sailing. You're calculating, not eccentric."

"Weak dollar, choppy Atlantic seas, longer European vacations. They really believe I didn't think about all of that. I am nautical miles ahead of them. Do I really care if any Americans go? We have our eyes on the future—right?"

"Absolutely. The World Championships in 2024 will be ours," said Skip. "You know, those reporters wish they had your money, and could spend it the way they wanted."

"We'll be away from the media once we're sailing. We can get in a lot of playing time, and relax with the Europeans. You know, relieve some stress before we get to Durres."

"Are you sure you want to keep that name, *The Ping*, after what Cheng Chui Ping did?"

"It's a done deal, painted on. Nobody's going to think of Sister Ping, or the Snakehead Queen as she was called. She died in prison five years ago. This is a luxury liner, not a cargo ship. If I named it the Golden Venture II, that would certainly set off some whistles and bells."

"She got thirty-five years you know, added Skip."

"She operated for a decade. She was greedy and bound to get caught. This is a one-off."

"A one-on and a one-off, you hope."

"Let's move on. I pulled some strings. We don't have to depart from Miami. We're leaving right from the shipyards in Port Everglades. It's just me and you, and the skeleton crew."

CHAPTER 3

THE PLAN

L ounging next to her pool, Kathy Hendrickson picked up her vibrating phone from atop her clear table.

"Hey sis, what's up?"

"I've got great news. You and Mark are on for the summer. Carl went with it, no problem."

"Wow. He must need a break from the situation too."

"He's fine. Anyway, Mark is out of his mind. He's scoped out the players at the clubs already, ordered a new paddle, and bought a new swimsuit. Also, he's been giddy about this table tennis themed cruise departing across the state from you in Miami. That might make a fun day trip. At least he could get a glimpse of the ship."

"That sounds cool. We'll talk soon."

Kathy opened her laptop and googled the unique venue. As she read on, her dormant adventure gene regenerated within. A few searches revealed the prior name of *The Ping* to be The *Challenger of the Seas*. Armed with a downloaded photo of the vessel, and not a clue to its precise location, she took off for a little reconnaissance. The hour and a half drive into Miami was one she had made many times, and she quickly eliminated the first class areas where the mega ships held court.

Back and forth along the Port of Miami, she scanned the harbors, periodically pulling over to lift her binoculars. Kathy meandered along the frontage roads, well south of the mainline carriers, and again stopped to search her phone for possibilities. Another option appeared, and she reversed course.

Now two hours into her search, and twenty five miles north of her original starting point, Kathy reached the maintenance yards of Port Everglades. The sun, biased to the west, sharpened the silhouettes along the waterfront. Slowing, Kathy's eyes alternated between the road and the yards to the right. She pulled over, holding up the image on the passenger seat. With the passenger side window lowered, she raised her field glasses. A patch of white paint danced in her lens, until she steadied her right elbow on the arm rest. Hazily, *The Ping of the Seas* converged into her view.

Directly west of the ship, a handful of cars sat in the parking lot. Kathy nestled her SUV among them, and secured a vantage point down the length of the dock. A white pickup truck was parked next to the open cargo door, beyond that, sat a security guard. Kathy watched, and read, periodically running her engine to infuse cool air. Two hours later, the guard folded up his card table and chair, collapsed his canopy, and carried them into the cargo opening. Two men followed him out, and the trio scrunched into the front seat of the truck. The gangway lifted, followed by the cargo door, and the truck approached the parking lot. Kathy slouched down in her seat, as the guard slid into his sedan, and drove off.

Kathy returned once a week for the next five weeks, varying her days. Her stays were short, as activity was light. Sometimes a truck sat next to the ship, and sometimes a couple men in a golf cart would rumble up the dock. Finally, on a Wednesday in mid-May, Kathy gathered up her courage. Her debut would not be without her large Shephard mix by her side.

Again burning a path across the state, Kathy pulled into the west lot, this time leading her companion out of the rear door. Seventy pounds of loyalty infused confidence into Kathy as the pair passed a neglected guard shed. Forty-two teeth would come to bear if the situation arose. Small puddles gave evidence of a passing shower, and under a flimsy canopy, the older security guard rested his head on a card table. Forty feet from him, a beat-up outhouse sat opposite his station. A screech from his two-way radio jolted him to an upright position. His blurry eyes fixated on the unusual visitors, and he rose as they got within conversation range.

"What on God's earth brings you in this area?"

"My grandfather was a longshoreman, and I used to hear the stories, the G-rated ones anyway. I miss him, so I try to find places that remind me of him."

"Well it's good you have your friend with you. This isn't Coral Gables you know. I'm Charlie."

"I'm Kathy, and this is Howie."

"Beautiful dog. How'd you pick this place out?"

"It just looked accessible, with a bit of mystery to it. I'm not interested seeing a bunch of giant cruise ships parked end to end. Security is all over the place anyway."

"Security is a good thing, it puts food on my table."

"You're right, definitely."

"So you're not a cruise person?"

"Not really," Kathy replied dishonestly. "I don't think I'd like to be on one of those huge ships. Too many people. I like the smaller ones, the off the beaten path stuff. Something like this is more my style. That name, The Ping of the Seas, is rather unusual. Where is it going?"

"They don't tell me much. I'm just a retired temporary worker. But I did hear, it was it was stopping in Lisbon, before heading to the Mediterranean. Practically all the crew and passengers will depart from across the pond. Most of the skeleton crew here will be arriving the morning it leaves. Right now a few workers are completing the final preparations. It's a specialty cruise, revolving around ping pong of all things."

"Oh I see, ping pong. Sounds interesting. Maybe I'll stop by next week. I don't want my guy here overheating."

"Be careful."

Kathy continued her walk past Charlie and snapped off a few quick images from her phone. She reset her activity counter and walked down the dock. From the gangway to the beginning of the dock, she calculated at six hundred feet. Once in her vehicle, she jotted down some notes in a small journal, and reviewed her images. For the boring one and a half hour drive home, she pondered the possibilities.

The following week, late morning on Friday, she again strolled along with Howie.

"Hello Charlie," she said cheerfully, as if they were now long-time friends.

"Good morning Kathy. You know, just an FYI, I won't be here until next Thursday, and then I will be back on Friday just for the morning."

"Sounds like it will be heading out."

"Yeah, on Saturday. They finally got the ping pong room finished except for the tables. The manufacturer is supposed to have them done just under the wire, and they will be rolled in on Thursday. The guy that's chartering this will be here, the skeleton crew will check in on Friday, and then it's hasta la vista."

"I might stop back here on Thursday, I know I have a few things going next week. Oh, and would it be possible to contact you? I own a small company and occasionally could use someone for a day here and there."

"Sure. Here's my cell in case I hook up with a different outfit. Oh, and can you stick around a minute while I run over to the men's room to get rid of a little coffee? There's never a soul in site, but just yell if you see anyone," Charlie said with a chuckle.

Setting her phone to stopwatch mode, Kathy watched the seconds tick…eighty, eighty-one, and then the door swung open.

"Thanks Kathy."

"You're welcome. See you next week," she said, walking back down the long dock, climbing into her SUV, and heading back towards Highway 75.

In Naples, Kathy typed *electric scooters* into the search bar of the *Amazon* page. Gray; the color doesn't matter. Quiet; that matters. Fifteen miles per hour, holds two hundred twenty pounds, runs for forty minutes on a charge. Her pointer glided to the quantity box; make it two. Four hundred plus dollars, overnight shipping. Very expensive disposable *Razor*s.

Kathy never struggled with word problems in grammar school. This one was elementary, and not one that would find its way into the math books, or tablets for that matter. A stretch of seven hundred feet spanned the distance from the parking lot to the ship's gangway. Mark would come in at about a hundred sixty-five with his backpack on. Forty-eight seconds would elapse at the conservative pace of ten miles per hour, roughly fifteen feet per second. That would leave thirty seconds to drop the scooters into the water, run up the ramp, and disappear.

The next day the doorbell rang, and Kathy stepped out into the warm Florida air.

"If you could just set them in front of the garage door," she said to the driver, illegibly scratching her signature on the weathered screen.

Kathy slid the boxes into the garage, and streamed some eighties tunes on her wireless speaker. The new scooter smell leapt out of the box as her knife pierced the clear tape. As comfortable with a screwdriver in her hand as a mouse, she breezed through the assembly, and the two-wheeled wonders began their overnight charge.

Forty-one year old women generally weren't seen zipping up and down their block on scooters. So Kathy threw the pair in the rear of her SUV and headed to the outskirts of Naples. Cannibalized by online sales, a shopping plaza sat empty, waiting for tenants, and new drivers. Kathy parked, and glanced around before she darted away. Strands of her straight blonde hair danced in the breeze, and the whine from the chain grabbed her attention. The expansive hull of The Ping would carom the din back to the dock. But years of night club duty required Charlie to have the conversation dialed up, and he would be in the *Porta Potty* anyway. Not that the enclosure would provide much soundproofing, but in the middle of his business, he'd be powerless. The second *Razor* performed flawlessly, and Kathy packed it up.

CHAPTER 4

THE PRE-RAMBLE

Mark walked over to the kitchen counter and peered around his mom who was checking the weather on her laptop.

"It's right around the corner, next Wednesday, the sixth. We'll take you to Great Falls, and then you'll make your connecting flight at O'Hare. Kathy will be waiting for you inside the Naples terminal."

"Is Dad going to take down the table in the garage while I'm gone?

"I didn't see any crooked letters on your report card."

The week crawled along for Mark, and finally Wednesday morning was upon him. To the Southeast, Great Falls International awaited, two and a half hours from home.

"If anything doesn't seem right, call us immediately," said Mark's dad.

"Kathy will have a yellow t-shirt and yellow cap on," said Candice.

Carl elected to wait in the car while Candice made sure Mark got through security. He wasn't going to check his paddles, he wanted them next to him, every minute. The handles and round surfaces attracted the attention of the TSA agent.

"Ping pong paddles eh. They must be special ones."

"Yes sir," Mark replied.

Uneventfully, Mark arrived in Chicago. Following the hectic changeover, he was airborne again, and after two hours, touched down in Naples. Kathy opened her arms when Mark walked towards her.

"You've grown up young man."

They stepped out into the parking lot of Southwest Florida International Airport, and the late afternoon air hung like wet curtains. Kathy pulled over a couple miles from the house, detouring into a drive-thru, and grabbed a bagful of tacos. Howie's deep barks penetrated into the garage as the door went up, and Mark was greeted with a flourish of licks as he entered the house.

"Let's head into the screened enclosure and eat at that table next to the pool."

"This is amazing," said Mark.

"We don't have to worry about critters, insects, debris—or alligators in here."

"Alligators?" asked Mark.

"I haven't seen any around here. But really, in some areas people do have the screens to keep the crocodilians out of the water. It's a different world down here. I mean I once ran with the bulls in Pamplona, but I'll pass on swimming with the gators. Tomorrow we can make a make a run to see some in the morning. You can stay in the pool all afternoon if you want."

After they finished their evening meal, Kathy showed Mark to his bedroom. Mark unpacked his essentials, played some games on his tablet, and fell asleep with it laying across his chest.

The next morning, Kathy finished her coffee as Mark woofed down a couple bowls of cereal.

"Ready guy?"

"Yeah."

The pair zipped along the *Tamiami*, the two lane highway, which skirts along the northern portion of the Florida Everglades.

Alligators flourish in the swampland that parallels the road. Kathy stopped at a visitor's center where they entered to gain a safer look at these prehistoric reptiles. A wooden walkway rose above a channel just yards from the highway. The pair strolled safely above them, and Mark counted off fifteen of the creatures.

"I'm afraid to take my eyes off of them," said Mark.

"You're fine up here, and most places, if you don't get too close," said Kathy. "We can hang out here for as long you want. Then we can head back."

Now back in Naples, Mark was fully entrenched in the pool, throwing a Frisbee for his pal and diving off the board. Equipped with a small scratch pad and pen, Kathy opened the dresser drawers in Mark's room and took notes on the neatly folded garments— waist 31, inseam 31, shirts medium. The mail was stopped, the bills were paid in advance. She called out to Mark.

"I made a couple sandwiches."

The icy air conditioning shocked Mark as he stepped inside after coarsely drying off.

"Can I eat outside?"

"Absolutely. I have to run out to the store. You can hang out here, but you shouldn't swim by yourself."

"No problem."

While in the shopping plaza parking lot, Kathy called Charlie.

"Hey, Kathy. What's up? Is something wrong?"

"Oh, no. I'm wondering if I might have dropped one of my earrings around your station. They're not that valuable, just sentimental. I don't think I'm going to be able to make it over there."

"I'll walk around and keep my eyes open."

"Thank you so much. Are you still going to be there tomorrow just in case?"

"Oh yeah. Everyone's in a tizzy because the ping pong tables are being flown in overnight and have to be anchored tomorrow morning. Nobody's going to be in a good mood."

"Crazy stuff. Thanks for looking for me."

"No problem my dear."

Kathy returned home with a couple department store bags in the trunk. A bag of snacks sat next to her on the passenger side floor. She glanced at the corner of the garage where the scooters sat, shrouded in canvas and charging. She walked in emptyhanded.

When Mark and Howie hit the pool again, Kathy grabbed the goods and closed the door to her bedroom. She removed the tags from the clothes she had purchased, efficiently layering them inside a new backpack. Clothes from her drawers were compressed into her pack. Personal items, incidentals, water bottles, and granola bars filled the outside pockets. With the packs now tucked in her closet, she boiled a pot of water, and threw some spaghetti in.

Mark, dried off and changed, sat down to the generously filled bowl of pasta, steaming in the center of the table.

"Hungry?" Asked Kathy.

"Starved."

"Hey your mom told me about that Ping of the Seas."

"Yeah. It's leaving Saturday."

"Maybe we can take a ride over there tomorrow and see if we can catch a look at it. It's north of Miami, less than two hours from here."

"That would be incredible."

"I'd like to get a really early start though."

"No problem."

Mark was out cold early from the day in the pool, and some help from the enormous helping of pasta. Kathy slipped into his room and removed a small case containing his paddles and balls. From his dresser, she grabbed his chargers and a book. The backpack was now complete. She tapped her *Uber* app, 7:00 a.m. confirmed.

CHAPTER 5

THE DASH

At 5:40 a.m. Mark was sound asleep. Howie jumped into the back seat of the SUV and Kathy sped off. It was twenty minutes to the kennel, and a couple more for a stop at the McDonalds drive-thru. Kathy pulled back into the garage at six-thirty and immediately ran upstairs to rouse Mark.

"C'mon guy. There's a breakfast sandwich for you. Bring your phone and tablet along with you."

Mark powered his breakfast, and at 6:55 a black SUV backed up into Kathy's driveway. With Mark in the bathroom, she opened the garage door, and loaded the scooters and backpacks into the rear of the vehicle.

"Day trip." Kathy said to the driver.

"Where's Howie," asked Mark as Kathy returned to lock the front door behind them.

"Doggie Day Care."

"Who's that?"

"I got an *Uber*. That drive gets to me sometimes."

It was a relatively quiet ride across Highway 75, and the driver turned into the sparsely populated parking lot.

"Right next to that pickup is fine," said Kathy.

The rear hatch opened, and a puzzled look came over Mark as Kathy lifted out both scooters and the packs.

"It's a surprise," she said.

The *Uber* driver sped away and Kathy pulled a smaller pair of binoculars out of her fanny pack. The backlighting from the sun, and the shade from the vessel made it difficult to see details, but Charlie appeared to be correct. Next to the cargo opening was a truck, its rear door rolled up all the way. In a few minutes, two men emerged. They entered the truck, rolled a table down a ramp, into the ship.

"What's going on?" asked Mark.

"They're loading the ping pong tables on board."

"I mean the scooters, the backpacks."

"I think we can slip onboard."

"Why don't we just ask?"

"They won't let us."

"You're not talking about—?"

"I've got you for two months. Once Mr. Kobara sees how good you are, you're gold. Legally they have to take care of us."

"My Dad will kill me."

"He doesn't have to know. The beauty of cell phones."

The truck blocked the view of Charlie's guard station. The outhouse sat visible in the sunlight on the left side of the dock. Six minutes later, the two men stepped into the truck again and wheeled another table inside.

"It's dark inside the truck. I can't tell how many tables are in there," said Kathy, poking her head around the left side of the pickup bed.

Finally after two more trips by the movers, the truck engine started, and the vehicle proceeded to the end of the dock, making a three point turn. Mark and Kathy moved around to the passenger side as the truck rumbled past them, and on to the frontage road. Charlie was now in plain view. He took a token look down the dock to the west, and began sauntering over to the blue portable toilet.

"Hit that ON switch," said Kathy. Push off and hit the throttle. Follow me and do what I do."

When the door closed behind Charlie, Kathy peeled off with Mark right behind. Kathy's head bobbed up and down, alternating glances between the outhouse and the seconds ticking on her wrist. She angled towards the ship, with Mark in close pursuit. The slight *Doppler Effect* of the approaching machines further amplified the chain noise, causing Charlie to turn his better ear to the west. Charlie though, was in the throws. Had the door hinges been on his left, he might have mustered up a peek. It was his last day anyway.

Just short of the gangway, the pair hit their brakes. Kathy dismounted, grabbed her *Razor* at both ends, and released it into the harbor waters. Astonished, but sensing the urgency, Mark followed suit. Small bubbles percolated atop of the calm waters as the two swiftly scampered up the gangway. Once onto the main deck, Kathy paused for a second, and took one last glance back at the outhouse. Quickly, they descended down one flight of stairs, eased open a cabin door, and locked it behind them. Immediately Kathy threw off her backpack and flopped on one of the beds, relieved. After a few minutes, she composed herself.

"The great room of table tennis is above us on the main deck, that's where they are doing the work now. There are guest rooms on that level, but probably with so few on board, the small staff may stay there. The captain, engineers, Mr. Kobara and company will likely stay in the suites on seven and eight. Kobara shouldn't relegate anyone down here, so we should be fine. But remain quiet tonight, keep your screens off."

Beads of sweat populated Kathy's face, and she walked over to the thermostat. She pressed the down arrow, and after twenty minutes there was no change.

"Did you bring my paddles?" asked Mark.

"Absolutely."

Kathy and Mark surfed the net and read throughout the day, pausing to partake in a couple granola bars and water. Mark, finally tired from his early rising, drifted off at 1:00 a.m. Candice paced, looking for relief from the muggy conditions. One level up, the rooms would have balconies, and at least a breeze could enter. She slipped her phone into her fanny pack and peeked out the cabin door. Low level, emergency type lighting provided enough illumination to navigate the hallway to the staircase. Hunched down, she ascended, temporarily stopping on the landing, half way up. She tiptoed up the next half flight of stairs and paused. Ahead of her was the bow, behind, the renovated table tennis room. The port side rooms would catch the southerly winds. As she made her move, a loud authoritative voice echoed from a distance.

"Halt!"

Kathy ran into the middle of the hallway, flung open a door and locked it behind her. She heard a jangle of keys, and the door next to hers opened. After ten seconds, it slammed, and the door handle of her room jiggled.

"You have no place to go but in the ocean. I have a master key and I am armed. Are you alone?"

"Yes," Kathy yelled.

"Lay down on the floor on your stomach in plain sight. Face away from the door, and put your hands behind your head. Yell out to me when you have done this."

The options were few. She was an excellent swimmer, but the jump overboard was daunting.

In a slow, deliberate, and defeated manner, she complied with the demands of the guard. With her heart beating rapidly against the floor, she again called out.

"Okay."

The guard located the master from his key ring, and drew his weapon from his holster. As he slid the key into the lock, his steel toed shoe contacted the bottom of the door, and it flew open.

"Stay down," he commanded.

He searched the bathroom, and the entirety of the suite.

"Lower your hands behind your back."

His rugged black boot moved firmly onto the small of Kathy's back. The safety clicked on his weapon, and he slid it into his holster. He carefully slid a set of plastic cable ties over her petite hands. Click by click, the restraints ratcheted, and he stopped.

"Up," he said, reaching underneath her left arm, assisting her to her feet.

"Are you alone?"

"Yes."

"Why are you onboard?"

"I was just trying to get a free trip to Europe."

Kathy was led with a loose grip on her arm to a small storage room. The guard unclipped her fanny pack and took it with him.

"I will be right back with a chair, and then I will figure out what to do with you," said the guard.

The guard went towards the bow of the ship, and grabbed his folding chair.

"Sit down."

He walked outside onto the deck out of earshot, and called his head of security.

"Max, I'm sorry to bother you at this hour, but we have a stowaway on The Ping of the Seas—a woman."

"Did you see anyone else?"

"No. She claims to be alone. I've got her info. Kathy Hendrickson from Naples. Here is her driver's license number. She appears harmless, and said she was just trying to get a free trip to Europe. "

"There's no video to review on that ship, outside of the great room. You can thank a few rich patrons for that one, wanting to have all the cameras removed. Hold on a few minutes while I do a background check on her."

"Got it," replied the guard. After a couple minutes his boss spoke.

"The only thing I see on her record is a fine from the National Park Service for rafting on a restricted portion of the Snake River. Maybe she really is just the adventurous kind. If we report this to the bosses at the corporate office, it won't reflect well on our security, and maybe affect our jobs. If we report this to the local authorities, it will be public. Who knows, everything is different these days. Homeland Security could be contacted, and we might not be able to leave right away. That Kobara guy would be out of his mind with a delay. He pays our company handsomely you know, and we wouldn't want to lose the next gig. The odds are, that she is alone, and that's it. Kobara, the captain, co-captain, and crew will be arriving at 7:00 a.m. I say, just put the ramp down, and tell her to get the hell out of there before anyone arrives. Oh, and tell her to keep her mouth shut about this."

"My instincts tell me you are right. Hopefully I scared her enough."

The guard walked back and opened the storage door. He grabbed a second chair and led Kathy out to the deck where they sat down across from each other.

"What are you thinking? An attractive young woman like yourself, alone on a vessel. Bad things could have happened to you. Did you think there would be no one watching a multi-million dollar ship? You had to have gotten on board when the ramp was attached, unless you had some special scaling equipment."

Kathy remained quiet, taking his onslaught in stride.

"Maybe you slipped past the guard or posed as a worker. Do you have a husband, kids? So many questions."

It remained a once in a lifetime opportunity for Mark. For Kathy, childhood endangerment could loom if things went awry. Kobara was crafty, but not wicked. Provisions had to be supplied. Mum was the word.

"Okay. I called the boss and you're not going to be charged. Before you walk the plank, I mean the gangway, answer this question. How did you get here?"

"*Uber.*"

"Alright. Stand up and turn around."

The guard snipped the plastic restraints and continued.

"Don't you have any luggage or personal belongings?"

"No. I'm a minimalist."

"Wow. Put these ties in your pocket. I don't want them showing up around here. Now get yourself a ride out of here. They can't drive up the dock, they have to wait in the parking lot."

Kathy tapped her app.

"I've got a ride."

The driver was due shortly. Kathy walked in front of the guard to the side of the ship. He noisily cranked down the ramp until it contacted the dock, and peered down towards the parking lot. A pair of headlights pierced the blackness.

"He's here," said Kathy.

"Behave yourself young lady."

"I will, and I really appreciate you not taking this any further."

It took five times as long to walk back along the dimly lit dock, as it did to navigate it using the scooters. The car ride back was long, dark and quiet. Back home, Kathy grabbed a couple hours sleep before rising early.

Repeatedly, Kathy sent the same text.

Mark, I was apprehended last night looking for a cooler room. I was just escorted off the ship, and wasn't arrested. I didn't mention anything about you. Nothing should happen to you if you want to get off. Strictly your decision.

Sprawled on his back, Mark slept coverless, as if he had stopped midstream making a snow angel. His phone listed to the outer side of his oversized left front pocket. The khaki material absorbed the urgent vibrations. Finally, as he shifted to his right, the oscillations stirred him. He looked over at the other empty bed. *Kathy had surely found another room*, he thought, removing his phone from his cargo shorts. Below the 9:45 a.m. at the top his screen, the text appeared. He sprung to his feet, pulled back the small curtain, and peered out the window. There was water between him and the dock, fifty feet of it.

He immediately texted Kathy, *we're moving.*

You still have time to run out and grab someone's attention. I know they would still return at this point.

To Mark, frantically running on deck, and desperately trying to get someone's attention, seemed weak and pathetic. The emasculating action would haunt him the rest of his life. How many times would he have to relive the decision to exit the ship? How many times would the words *what if* put him into a daydream? The moment of reckoning in the great room still loomed ahead of him. Appearing in front of Scott without the physical presence of his aunt would be unnerving, but excitement and intrigue awaited, dwarfing the decision to flee. The longer Mark debated, the more the ship's progress cemented his decision. With an extra serving of intestinal fortitude, he confirmed the most difficult decision of his life.

I'm staying.

Great decision. I am so happy for you, and I am here for you every second. We must decide if and when we are going to come clean to your parents. If you choose to tell them the truth, please let me know beforehand. Oh, and don't be alarmed when you open your backpack. I got you a bunch of new clothes.

Mark's decision quelled the chaotic urgency of the moment. He was now committed to an adventure. One far away from the constrictive confines of the garage. An exotic summer camp, on a vast ocean, where he hopefully could pursue his passion.

THE REVEAL

The Ping was now cruising eastbound, disappearing from the Miami harbor. Mark again looked out to see only water and sky. He flopped on the overstuffed bed and looked for any *Twitter* updates Mr. Kobara may have posted.

No connection available. The last bar on his signal strength meter flickered, and disappeared. He searched for a Wi-Fi connection —nothing.

Miami faded away, along with his signal. In a weird way, the loss of this cyber connection with his aunt, seemed as devastating as losing her physical absence. He was unable to seek advice, or express his emotions. In Naples, Kathy tried to message him, and realized that he was probably beyond Miami's cellular range. Mark plucked a book and a couple granola bars out of his backpack and leaned against his headboard.

Early that afternoon, the snappy pops of plastic balls echoed in the expansive room retrofitted for table tennis. Scott Kobara and his manager Skip, rallied back and forth rhythmically and relentlessly. Scott was fit and agile for his age. Skip was twenty years his junior, and an accomplished player with a USATT rating of 1900. Whatever country Scott visited, Skip was along, to make sure Scott had a sparring partner. Besides managing the Hawthorne Center, Skip helped Scott make the cruise a reality.

Mark picked up the TV remote and game show laughter erupted from the wall mounted screen. He scrambled for the volume button and surfed. Channel 100 revealed a wide angled view of a large room, populated with ping pong tables. Two individuals were rallying in the far corner. *The great room!* Mark hit the plus button, and the view zoomed in on the end table. The competence of the now recognizable pair was on display. Mark's longing for food temporarily subsided, and he absorbed himself into the action.

Their footwork could be better, but not bad for old guys. The loops aren't killer, and Skip's got good range. Emerging today was risky, tomorrow they would be well beyond the point of no return. Another twenty-four hours was unbearable. Mark removed his protective case from its well-cushioned spot, tied his shoes, and stretched. Mustering up all his courage, he cracked his door, and repeated, *stay strong, you belong.*

All sense of security vanished when Mark stepped out of his room. He might as well have been walking out into the ocean. His sweaty right palm reluctantly let go of the lever, and he quietly made his way to the staircase. He remained steady upon reaching the main deck, and proceeded down the hallway. A small square window in the entrance door allowed him to view most of the playing area. *I belong* he again whispered, pulling his shoulders back, and he reached for the handle.

Mark cracked the door and stepped inside. The drone of the balls pounding on the surface of the table echoed throughout the room. The sweet sound, and the ambiance of the room left him awestruck. The tinted windows eliminated all glare, and provided a look of infinity out to the ocean. Baffles and light tubes diffused the light naturally and evenly over all sixteen tables. For five seconds Mark was lost in the aura. As Scott turned to retrieve a wayward shot from Skip, he caught Mark's profile out of the corner of his eye. Quiet overcame the room, and Scott could now discern that an adolescent was along for the ride.

The voice of Scott Kobara reverberated off the glass.

"What the—?" "There are no kids on this ship."

Comprised of wood and rubber, Mark's security blanket hung from his right hand. Squeezing the most powerful weapon he owned, Mark drew strength from the handle of his bat, and spoke.

"I'm Mark Linderman. I've always wanted to meet you."

"Get over here. Who is with you and how did you get onboard?"

Now, tentatively stopping ten feet away from Scott, Mark replied, "I am alone. I snuck past the guard."

"This is absurd. This cannot be happening. Where do you live?"

"Montana."

"Do your parents know about this?"

"No."

"Outrageous. The captain must be playing a joke on me."

"It looks like he came to play some pong," quipped Skip with a wry smile.

"I think I'm pretty good," added Mark.

"Everyone thinks they are good," barked Scott. "I am aware of every young player in the entire United States ranked above 2000, and I can say definitively, there are none from Montana. So when you get above that level, send me a postcard."

The opportunity for Mark to switch on his light sabre and electrify Scott, appeared to be fading, so Mark spoke up again.

"Just give me the chance to show you. That's all I'm asking."

"There can be major repercussions from this. Maybe your parents should have to foot the cost of the cruise. You would be paying that back for years and years to come. How about being quarantined to a small room down below. I'm only beginning. Skip, keep him right where he is. I'm going outside on the deck to think about this, and then going up to the bridge to talk to the captain. We're probably only a hundred miles out."

As Scott disappeared, Skip said to Mark,

"He can be a bit edgy sometimes. I don't approve of what you did, but I must admit, it's pretty gutsy. Here, hurry up and hit some balls with me because you might not get another chance."

Skip tapped an easy serve over and Mark imparted a healthy rotation of top spin with a backhand flick. Within seconds, the pace of rallying ramped up exponentially. Mark delivered loops that were increasingly difficult for Skip to manage. Mark began blocking Skip's slams and rocketing smashes past him. Both players were lost in the moment when Skip stopped.

"Excuse me a minute," said Skip.

Skip reached into his sport bag, pulled out his two-way radio, and stepped outside.

"Have you reached the bridge yet?"

"No."

"Stop. Stop. Turn around. Get back down here!"

"Did he jump off?"

"Just get down here."

Scott made his way back into the great room to see Skip and Mark standing at ends of the table with paddles in their hands.

"I have a stowaway, and now an employee that doesn't follow instructions."

Before Scott could think of physically intervening, Skip put the ball in play and the two were back at it. Scott's outrage began to melt away with each precise and deadly shot he witnessed. A smash, a loop, a block, a chop, a lob, a complete arsenal, executed with ease and grace.

Skip turned to Scott, "I can't put a rating on him, but I think 2000 disappeared from his rear view mirror quite a while ago.

"How old are you?" asked Scott.

"Sixteen,"

"So who do you practice and play with?"

"I just use ball machines in my garage."

"That's impossible. Robots only augment one's game. How much do you practice?"

"On school days, five hours. On weekends, or during the summer, usually eight to ten. I take some non-playing time to watch matches and instructional videos, like on your website, which is really sweet. I hadn't visited it for a while, and then I read about this cruise."

"Haven't you craved playing with a live partner?"

"Yeah. Nobody plays around me, and the kids are down on me for not playing other sports. There's no clubs around."

"This is quite the venue to emerge from obscurity."

Scott and Skip alternated hitting against Mark, and remained completely confounded by his prodigious play. The cat-like reflexes, the poise, and the answers for every shot thrown at him.

"It's two o'clock." said Scott. "Why don't we go upstairs and get some lunch?" Where have you been hiding out on the ship Mark?"

"I found a room on level four."

"That's steerage. Grab your things and head up to eight. We can sit by the pool, have lunch, and we'll find you a different room."

Scott's attitude did a one eighty in minutes. Mark entered his room and began collecting his few loose items. He walked over to make the bed Kathy attempted to sleep in, and noticed her backpack next to it. It wasn't anything he wanted to explain to anyone, and something he didn't want to toss overboard. He envisioned the pack stuck in the stomach of a sea mammal, or it washing up on shore, and someone extracting some recoverable DNA. He rifled through the feminine attire and personals, checking for any personal information, and slung it over his shoulder.

Mark climbed the stairs to the top level of the ship. His solution was right in front of him. A place seldom visited, the lifeboats. The door was unlocked leading into the orange enclosure. Mark walked to the rear, and underneath a large pile of life preservers, he buried the pack. He descended down a level, where centered the in the open area, was a sky-blue swimming pool surrounded by a sea of chaise lounges. Scott and Skip sat at a table under an umbrella in the terraced area.

"Scott, what are you going to tell the captain?" asked Skip.

"That there was some kind of mix up."

Mark came into view, and Scott waved, calling out.

"Over here, have a seat."

Completely famished, Mark sat down.

"Order whatever you want."

"Could I get two double cheeseburgers?" asked Mark.

"Absolutely," replied Scott.

"So where are you from in Montana?" asked Skip.

"Oh a little town called Chinook."

"And how did you make it all the way down here?"

"I flew, and then I got a ride."

"What rubber do you use on your paddle?" asked Scott, changing the subject.

At that point the co-captain walked by to pick up some food for him and the captain.

"Who's this?" Asked the co-captain abruptly. "There weren't any kids on the manifest."

"You mean you didn't get my communication. He was a last minute sign on."

"Very funny. Where are his parents? This is serious you know."

"I am his guardian. Really, I sent you guys the info."

"BS."

"Oh, the rubber I use is *Mark V*," said Mark, as he fixated on the approaching waitress.

The swaying tray came to a rest next to the table. Two cheeseburgers, a heap of fries, and a large cola were set down in front of Mark. The ravenous teen could have downed his meal in a couple minutes, but used enough restraint to finish in a civilized manner.

"Skip, do you remember the rooms on seven which were not taken?" asked Scott.

"A couple of the Veranda Suites. I'm pretty sure 715 was one of them."

"C'mon, let me show you where you will be staying," said Scott.

The pair headed down the stairs to the seventh level while Skip stayed behind. Scott opened the door and bright sunshine graced the expansive suite. The ability to hit the little white ball had changed things. In less than two hours, Mark had transitioned from a stowaway into a special guest.

"Check it out," said Scott with a smile.

"Wow!"

"If you need anything let me know. There's very few people on board. If anyone asks you any questions, just tell them I'm your guardian. The Wi-Fi's good up here so you'll be able to text and browse. I'm in 701 at the front of the ship, and Skip in is 702. We will either be in our rooms, eating, or downstairs playing. If we aren't down there, help yourself to the robot."

Mark took out his phone and charger. In just a few minutes he was up and running. Immediately he began to text Kathy.

Aunt Kathy. I am texting you from a suite on the seventh level. It has a huge bed, a refrigerator, big flat screen TV, and a sofa in a separate room that leads out to the balcony. Mr. Kobara was very angry when he saw me. He threatened to not let me play table tennis, and to charge us for the cruise. When he was away, I hit balls with his club manager, and everything changed. They fed me whatever I wanted, and gave me this room. Mr. Kobara told me to tell people he was my guardian if anyone asked.

I knew you would do it, Texted Kathy. *You should be safe now, because there is no way Scott wants anything to happen to you.*

I'm going down to practice in the great room where the tables are, it is unreal.

I can imagine. Get in touch anytime if you need to talk, and to just let me know how it's going.

Okay.

Mark walked into the sitting area and flopped on the sofa to test the comfort. He ventured out onto the balcony where the endless ocean and sky briefly held his attention. There were vacant tables and idle ball machines calling him. He marched downstairs directly to the practice room with the multi-ball robot. The netting that surrounded the far half of the table, insured that a player rarely had to do the menial task of picking up any balls. It was a continuous collection system that recirculated the struck balls right back into the robot hopper. This was the Space Shuttle version compared to his garage. After some experimentation, Mark was back in full training mode. He wasn't used to such ideal conditions, the lighting, temperature, the consistency. He cooked up a quick routine, and became immersed.

Upstairs, back on the pool deck, Scott and Skip conversed.

"So what is your evaluation of this kid?" asked Scott.

At this point the captain walked over to their table.

"What are you trying to pull off?" He asked.

"Hey, C'mon. I did what I was supposed to do."

"BS. You're lucky. Well I should say we're lucky that this isn't one of the major lines, and that I have some connections. There's a lot of explaining to do when there's an extra passenger disembarking. I am going to need all of his information."

"No problem," said Scott.

The captain headed back to his post and Scott addressed Skip.

"Okay, go ahead with *your* appraisal of Mark. I'm sure it will mirror mine."

"In a word, versatility, and he's got great economy of movement."

"I agree. Go ahead, elaborate, said Scott."

"His game seems to have a lot of gears, and he is very adaptable. Pure talent, unadulterated, and unformed by human hands. He hasn't had a strong coach who imposed his style on him. When I was immediately ready to classify him as an all-round attacker, he would begin to morph into a counter driver. Then like he was toying with me, he would do some close to the table defender type play. He's obviously a student of the game, and if he was practicing against humans, they wouldn't have had the patience for him to develop all these styles. He's the Swiss Army Knife, and the box of chocolates."

"Enough with the metaphors or idioms, or whatever they call them. So it seems he can confound anyone trying to scout him. That's a strong asset to have, not being able to be classified. A lot of kids have their lane picked for them by their coach."

"So what do you think Scott?" asked Skip.

"I agree, totally. I never thought being *self-taught* could be such an asset. He doesn't seem to be caught up in outside distractions. A lot of young players move on to other things when they don't have someone pushing them. This kid is a lone wolf, so self-motivated, but that can change. We would have two or so years to try to develop him into a world class player. Just imagine what Koji and the *Zengmaster* could do with Mark's raw talents. After we return, if we can get him up to New York, Koji can give the final evaluation. We would have a little more than a month to work with him before he has to go back to Montana. Of course that's assuming his parents don't crash this whole thing."

"I'm with you on that," said Skip. "It should be an easy sell to Mark."

"Yep. I don't think Mark would need any persuasion to stick around indefinitely. His dad is not happy with him. Koji loves the game, and his kindness and captivating nature should overwhelm Mark. Anyway, I am out of my mind right now with the potential. My rational side says there's a lot to pull off before things even get to that point. Let's go downstairs and hit some."

The pair strolled into the great room and there was Mark fully engaged and oblivious to anything outside of his practice room. Skip went over to the window and got his attention.

"Take a break from the robot and hit some balls with Scott. Oh, and take it easy on him," said Skip with a chuckle.

Scott and Mark rallied back and forth in a physically negotiated and casual pace. Even so, at half speed, Mark's loops were like frogs bounding off a hot sidewalk. Skip stepped in, and the three rotated in round robin fashion well into the afternoon.

"Meet us in the restaurant on seven at the rear of the ship at six o'clock. It looks fancy, but if you don't have anything decent to wear, don't worry about it. It will probably only be us there. Oh, and anytime you want to use the pool, go right ahead," said Scott.

Mark discovered a nicer pair of shorts and a collared shirt in his pack. He proceeded down to the laundry area on the fourth level, ironed, and came back up to shower. The now presentable teen strolled into the restaurant. White table cloths and upholstered wooden chairs spanned the width of the vessel. All this awaited, merely for sneaking onto a ship, and smacking the small white balls around.

A woman approached him as he entered the elegant room.

"You must be Mark. Welcome. My name is Maria and I will be your hostess and waitress this evening. I can seat you at any one of those tables along the windows. They have the nicest view. Scott and Skip had some business to take care of, so they just grabbed a couple sandwiches and said for you to order whatever you would like. May I suggest the sixteen ounce New York strip? I can accompany that with a baked potato doused in butter, along with some baby carrots. Scott's got you covered."

"That really sounds great. Thank you."

Mark was quickly closing the calorie deficit he had developed, as he chowed down the Texas sized meal.

"How about some chocolate cake?" asked Maria.

"Yes please."

Mark finished, and now fully satisfied, headed back to his suite. He debated doing some head to head battle with one of the bots, but ultimately, sprawled out on the luxurious bed and checked out the movie offerings.

CHAPTER 7

THE U-TURN

Nightfall encompassed the Atlantic, which had been relatively calm so far. Scott combed over his options regarding the young sensation which fell into his lap. Immediately getting Mark into an intensive training program became the priority. If Mark showed promise, convincing his parents to allow him to remain in New York was the next hurdle.

Lying on his back in bed, Scott's watch chirped at midnight. The Europeans might not react favorably to a whiz kid not registered for the cruise, especially under the presumed guardianship of the host. A kid who might even be able to beat some of them. Getting Mark off the ship in Lisbon and sending him back would get interesting. A driver's license and library card wouldn't cut the mustard, and if the media got a hold of it, it certainly would go viral. The captain's connections were stateside, internationally, it could be another story.

Inside his luxury suite, Scott walked over to the safe, punched the keypad, and pulled the door open. Among a few personal items, sat a tightly bundled stack of bills. He grabbed the currency, and stuffed it into the oversized right pocket of his cargo shorts. Before proceeding up to the bridge, he walked outside for a minute, and leaned against the outer railing, staring into the abyss. He continued up to level eight, and then up a narrow set of stairs, leading to a secure metal door. Raising his right hand, he wrapped with his knuckles in coded fashion. The captain recognized the sequence, and pressed his face against a small security window. Years of saltwater air, and lack of use, caused the hinges to groan as he ratcheted the door towards him.

"What brings you up here at this hour?" asked Captain Clarke as he let Scott in. "I hope you don't have someone else you would like to declare as a passenger."

"No, I couldn't sleep so I thought I would come up and chat. Don't you have two guys up here?"

"She's on auto pilot now. The staff captain is getting some sleep, and there's no trouble on the horizon for as far as the eye can see. That's a good thing when you don't have a giant ship, and you've got a couple of people that want to play ping pong in the middle of the ocean."

"What about the technical guys, where do they hang out?"

"We have a chief engineer and the general engineer. They're up here sometimes, but end up all over the place. They're usually down in the propulsion area."

"Well, it would be great to get a tour someday, if that is allowed."

"In this instance, it's no problem. I think Jeff is doing the night shift tonight. I can have him text you, and you guys can arrange something."

"That would be fantastic."

Immediately Scott's phone buzzed.

Anytime is fine. Just text me to make sure I am not involved with anything.

Great. How about in fifteen minutes.

Sounds like you're anxious. Meet me at the middle staircase landing on the fourth level.

Scott hung around the bridge for about ten minutes before easing towards the door.

"Thanks for chatting. I'm going to walk around outside for a little while."

Scott walked as quickly as he could to the meeting point.

"C'mon down," said Jeff, leading him down through a series of secure areas. Before they entered the lowest level, they stopped in a small control room.

"Pretty impressive so far," said Scott."

"Yeah, it all comes together and works pretty well," replied Jeff.

Scott reached into the front pocket of his baggy cargo shorts and slapped the stack of one hundred dollar bills on a desk.

"There are one hundred of these in there, and that is most of what I brought onboard. Please pardon me ahead of time for asking. I am not judging you for even giving this any consideration. I just need a favor. I need you to mysteriously transform the temperatures onboard from the low seventies into the eighties ASAP. You know me, I will additionally compensate you when we get back home.

"That's quite a sum of money. From what I detect you are saying, is that you would like it a bit uncomfortable onboard, and why may I ask?"

"Okay. Let me level with you. I need to get that kid off the ship. The captain would probably turn around, but the charter company would be livid, having the ship return because of a stowaway on board. I need the failure to look legitimate and completely random. The ship must be forced to return to the States for repairs, quick repairs. I want the ship to be able to head back out to the Mediterranean, ASAP."

Without a word, Jeff took out a key, nodded. He stuck the stack of bills into a locker, and led Scott back upstairs before diving into his documentation. Scott returned to his room, and finally managed to finally fall asleep. Meanwhile, Mark was up at 8:00 a.m., grabbed an egg sandwich at the restaurant, and headed down to great room to challenge the robots. He eased into his usual warm-up routine and a few beads of sweat began to populate his forehead. The warmer, the better.

Scott awoke on his own and sensed a touch of stuffiness in his suite. He was devoid of covers which were clumped at the foot of his bed. The low contrast display on the thermostat was unreadable from afar. He climbed out of bed and a pair of sevens graced the display. It was warm outside, as it can be leaving from Florida. Mother Nature's air conditioning was not in the forecast this week. Scott cleaned up and walked over to the restaurant for a pastry and cup of coffee to go.

"Good morning Scott. It feels a bit warm in here this morning, especially when you are moving around," said the woman behind the counter.

"Yeah, that sun can really beam in."

Scott headed downstairs to the main deck and entered the toasty great room. Mark was still battling as patches of sweat populated his forehead. Scott walked over to the practice area.

"Good Morning. Why don't you take a break and we can relax outside? Skip said was going to come down here this morning, so save some energy for him."

The pair leaned back in their lounge chairs, and took in the warm ocean breeze.

"What do you think of the great room?" asked Scott.

"It beats my garage."

"The glass panels are high tech. They're called dynamic transitional panes, which change the amount of light they admit, depending on the outside conditions. Kind of like those fancy eyeglasses, but giant and thick. They keep the illumination ideal, and help keep the temperature constant, except for today maybe, which is quite strange. It's all about making the game a better experience."

"That's cool. I'm into physics," said Mark.

"You've chosen the greatest game, you know," continued Scott. "You can play it year round, it's inexpensive, and great for the mind and body. It's international. I have played at clubs in many countries, and each match ended in a handshake. If you make a mistake in a game, there's no time to dwell on it, you're on to the next point. Instant redemption awaits."

"My dad never talked like that."

"It's too bad he isn't crazy about your passion. It's something you guys could do together"

"He thought it was cute when I was small, but when I got older and passed up playing the popular sports, he just kind of withdrew from me. My Mom is cool about it though."

At that point Skip emerged onto the deck.

"Hi guys, taking a break I see. I don't blame you. I just came from seven where I got some breakfast. They were chirping about the temperature up there."

"I'm heading up there to change and grab my paddle. You guys spar a bit, and I should be back down in a half hour or so," said Scott.

Mark and Skip headed back inside for some intensive play while Scott ascended two levels up and stopped into the restaurant.

"What's this I hear about it being warm onboard?"

"Don't you feel it?" asked Maria.

"You know us old guys, we need our sweaters when it's under seventy five outside," joked Scott.

Scott walked into his room and peeked at the thermostat. Smugly, he stared at the display, and as if his mind was controlling it, the seven transitioned to an eight. The captain would have to capitulate at some point. Pounding the table for a return might attract attention Scott didn't need. Scott donned his shorts, grabbed his sport bag, and headed back downstairs. When he entered, Skip was entirely drenched, while a wet sheen coated Mark's skin.

"Here, you get over here. He put me through the spin cycle, and I'm ready to be hung out to dry. It's impossible to play for very long in here," exclaimed Skip.

Scott tried to be low key about the discomfort, but threw in the towel after ten minutes. On the other side of the table, Mark was unfazed, appearing ready to play all day. The windows only went so far to moderate the heat. Without cool moving air, the room was unusable, for most.

"I'm going up and find out what's going on," said Scott.

Skip accompanied Scott back upstairs, in desperate need of a shower, while Mark stayed behind for another session against his automated opponent. After cleaning up, Scott slugged his way up to the bridge.

"Mr. Kobara. I think I might know why you are up here to visit," said the Captain.

"I heard a few people expressing some discomfort."

"Well I've got both my crack engineers down below working on it. It appears to be specific to the air conditioning system. It's odd that I didn't get any warning lights up here. I will keep you posted."

"Thanks. I guess these older ships can have their quirks."

Despite the conditions, Mark alternately battled the robot and then programmed a new multi-ball configuration into the software. After a couple hours he was ready for a shower and a big plate of food. When he got into his room he sent Kathy a text.

Hey. Everything's okay. Something is wrong with the air conditioning so Scott and his friend Skip did not play very long. I just practiced with this super robot that had tons of programs. I'll probably go in the pool, eat, and then just watch TV tonight.

It's great to hear from you. You might have gotten in more playing time in here at the clubs, but I know this will work out for you. At least you're having a unique experience. Stay cool.

Scott and Skip relaxed at a small table in one of the shaded areas surrounding the pool.

"What's up on the A/C problem?" asked Skip.

"Well the Captain is keeping me in the loop. They are focusing on one of the generators, and one of the electrical busses behind a panel."

"Sounds pretty major."

"Yeah. Everyone will have the option of sleeping out on their balcony from now on. The Captain said cots would be delivered and placed out on everyone's veranda. All of the crewmembers are staying on five, so they will be okay." At that point Mark walked by to go for a swim.

"Hey there. Do you want to join us for dinner out here about six?" asked Scott.

"Sure."

Mark felt strange being the only one in the pool on a large ship, so he cut his swim short, and cleaned up for dinner. Scott and Skip were already munching on some carrot sticks when Mark sat down?"

"Are we the only three passengers?"

"Yes, for now," said Scott. "When we arrive in Lisbon there should be a total of forty eight getting on board, so things will be different. With this ship dedicated to table tennis, there's not a lot of special activities. There will be music, games, and other entertainment, so only about thirty more crew members will board. Still, that's a tiny number compared to the large ships."

"Is your club still open while you two are on this cruise?"

"Absolutely. It slows down a bit in the summer, except we do have more travelers from around the country, and the world, who come to play. Koji and another guy help me out."

"Koji Yamaguchi?"

"You've heard of him?"

"Yeah. He was the American who came close to defeating Ying in the 1997 world championship. They were using the thirty-eight millimeter balls, and the games were played to twenty-one."

"Impressive. That happened before you were born. Those old balls spun like a dentist's drill. Koji is still great, in so many ways. I think I'm going to hit it early tonight. How about you Skip?"

"Yeah. The heat's wearing on me."

Mark traipsed off to his room. After a couple hours, his outstretched arm released the remote, and he drifted off. Outside on his balcony, the blanket on the empty cot flapped in the wind. Just about that same time, Scott's walkie-talkie squawked, rousing him out of his sleep.

"Captain Clarke here. Come up to the bridge in fifteen minutes for a meeting." Scott and Skip met outside of their rooms and walked up together. The pair entered the bridge to find the Captain, Staff Captain, Chief Engineer, and General Engineer all standing together.

"Gentlemen, I have very bad news for us all. As you have noticed, it has gotten very warm in here over the last couple days. A catastrophic failure has occurred in the air conditioning section of the ship. A large generator has failed, and as a result of the surge, there is a burned section of wiring behind the main electrical bus. Also the surge took out a control circuit board in the computer that monitors the current that is flowing. Jeff here, our general engineer, is our air conditioning expert. He has been living on the phone with our Engineering Department at our headquarters in Florida."

"Normally, it could be possible, especially with such a small number of guests, to maybe move to another vessel in Lisbon. Of course, this ship is now one of a kind, we cannot substitute it out. The Atlantic was kind to us last night, but as we enter the Mediterranean in the heat of the summer, it will be a different story. Without air conditioning, the suites, great room, and the restaurants, will become unbearable."

"So what are you saying Captain?" asked Scott.

"Well, we are only scheduled for a short turnaround in Lisbon due to the small number of passengers and crew. We can't stay docked there for a couple days, and our alternatives are not attractive. We would have to find a different port with short notice, and fly in the parts and the personnel to expedite the repairs. There's always a chance that we would need something else which would delay things. Port Everglades has everything there. I say we cut bait right now and head back to the states. We can be back in Miami in less than two days, and the repairs should take two days, or less. If this was only a week long cruise, we'd be out of business, but if we act fast we can still salvage a little more than two weeks in the Mediterranean. I'm sure most, if not all the guests would still sail."

"Well, the best laid plans," said Scott. "I say do what we have to. Don't worry about the patrons, I'll make sure they are well compensated. Once the Europeans are full of food and drink, and the sixteen tables are all humming, this will just be a bump in the road. I'll have Skip here make sure everyone is informed and has hotel rooms in Lisbon if they left home already. If anyone has trouble changing their flights, get them first class seats."

"Okay Scott. I'm calling our office and doing the *U-turn* right now."

The meeting broke up, with Scott and Skip settling in for the rest of the night before a busy day of correspondence with the Europeans. The next day Scott took a midday break from his tasks and headed down to the very balmy great room. Mark was at with his usual fury, battling the robot, covered in sweat, and oblivious to his surroundings. Scott went up to the glass and signaled to him to step outside.

"Sit down. The air conditioning problem is forcing the ship back to Florida for repairs. It should arrive there tomorrow and then head to Lisbon, arriving almost a week late."

"So what about me?" asked Mark.

"I would really like to have you along, but you don't have any identification. Both of your parents, or a notarized signature of the absent parent are required for you to obtain a passport. It sounds like your father would have no part of this. The charter company and I could get in a whole lot of trouble housing you on this ship without proper documentation."

"I really don't want to go back. I want to play with the great European players."

"I totally understand. I'm as crazy about the game as you are. I would love you to stay, but I don't make the rules. Somebody needs to be waiting for you when you disembark."

"My aunt, actually. I was spending the summer with her in Naples."

"Great. When the ship docks, I want to speak with her. If you don't have to tell your parents anything, wait until I speak with her."

"Okay."

Mark fumed, *I hate air conditioning, and the machines that make it.*

The ship's vents were starved of cool air, but Mark vented against the robots, and with a vengeance. His resolve was etched in his paddle like a stone tablet, and was imprinted onto each ball. His frustration with his impending exit, was evident in every stroke. He continued to lose himself in a world that had separated him from his dad, classmates, and society in general.

The following day, with five hours left before The Ping was set to dock, Scott knocked on Mark's door. He stepped up the rapping with no response. The pool and restaurant were both vacant. Scott marched his way down and surveyed the empty great room. He had now covered Mark's four main hangouts on the ship. One of the elevators was said to be quirky. Scott preferred doing the stairs anyway, as a means to help keep himself in excellent shape. He walked over and pressed the button on the first one. The doors opened, and no passenger. On the other end of the ship he was greeted with the same results. He called up Skip on his radio.

"Hey Skip, can you get hold of the captain or co-captain and see if you can get a master key for the suites?"

"What's up?"

"I can't find Mark. Get the key and meet me at his room."

Skip hustled down and met Scott in the hallway. Scott rapped on the door with no response. With a signal from Scott, Skip inserted the key and opened the door slowly. The empty bed was made and the room was tidy. There were no personal belongings in view. They looked in the bathroom and under the beds. The sliding doors leading out to the balcony were open.

"You don't think…? He was upset. No way. No one would ever recover from this. I would be ruined."

"Why would he have his things with him, if he did?" asked Skip.

"Good question. I told him to tell his aunt approximately when we would be arriving. If we don't find him and she is waiting, we have a lot of explaining to do. We have to check every room that is not occupied, the theater, the other restaurant, lounge, laundry room, exercise room, everywhere. Grab a diagram of the ship. Make sure all the life boats are there. I heard it takes special training to lower those, but I wouldn't put anything past him. We can't sail if we don't find him, and my reputation would be trashed. If we sail with him onboard, I could face charges. He has me held hostage."

"I know there are one hundred and fifty rooms. At one minute per room, that adds up to two and one half hours. I don't think that's part of my job description," said Skip.

"Get Maria to help out. That will expedite things. Keep the

captain and company out of the loop until we have to let them know he's missing. This would really set them off. Contact me when you have completed that search."

Two hours elapsed and Skip pushed his radio button to alert Scott.

"Nothing here. We marked every room on this printout that we checked. All the life boats are intact. The doors leading to the floors below level four are all secured. I checked the restaurants, kitchens, lounges, laundry area, bathrooms, and library. I went backstage in the theatre and checked the area above the stage, under it, and the rooms behind it."

The three met up on the main deck now with just a couple hours before the ship would reach Miami when it dawned on Skip.

"The lifeboats. Maybe he ducked inside one of them."

Four of the oversized emergency pods clung to the rear of the ship on the seventh level.

"You two take the starboard side, and I'll take the port side," commanded Scott.

Scott peered into the unsecured door of the first boat and a window on the ocean side was open. Sitting in the rear of the pod, next to the stack of life preservers was Mark, writing on a medium sized tablet.

"What are you doing?" asked Scott. "We've got a search party out looking for you, and we're only a couple hours from shore. Did you call your aunt?"

"Yeah, she will be here."

Scott's voice squawked out to Skip.

"I found him. He's sitting in one of the lifeboats, writing."

"Why did you choose this spot?"

"It's kind of a like my garage, isolated. Being inside one of these helped me picture what it might be like alone on the ocean. I started taking notes for a possible book."

"About what?"

"I sneak onto a ship with only a few people on board, and it catches fire the middle of the Atlantic. The fire separates me from everyone, and I have to lower this lifeboat down by myself. Then I just drift alone for days."

"How did the fire start?"

"It starts in the air conditioning section. A big transformer shorts out."

"Interesting," said Scott, taken aback by the uncanniness of the plot. "I'll have to read it when it's done."

Mark grabbed both backpacks, and accompanied Scott out of the pod and over to the poolside lounge area seven.

"Have a seat. What are your plans again for the remaining weeks of the summer?

"I'm going to play at a couple clubs in Naples."

"That's nice that you have family you can visit."

"What about you?" asked Mark. "I mean, do you have family?"

"No. No brothers or sisters. I never married. I guess that's why I do crazy things like this cruise. I was close once during college, but I began travelling so much it never happened."

"My aunt never got married. She liked to do wild things when she was younger."

"Anyway." Continued Scott. "Those clubs in Naples are likely to have some wily veterans who have learned how to adapt to their physical limitations. Older guys that have those crazy pips and anti-spin on their paddles. They punch knuckle balls back at wide angles, and fast, before you have time to set up.

They keep you on the defensive more than you are used to. Their style gives the kids and intermediate players fits, but that usually only goes so far. There should be some fine modern style players there, but nothing like around the big cities. That's generally where the top players congregate."

Scott captivated Mark for the next ninety minutes with his knowledge of the game. The changes, his club, foreign clubs, racket technology, players, and strategy. Only a week ago Mark was fired up to have the opportunity to play against live competition in Naples. Now, he had sampled something much more fascinating. Playing with the older guys in Florida paled in comparison to playing against the best in the world on a ship.

"Hey, look at that skyline," said Scott as Miami came into view.

The buildings meant nothing but the end of the journey for Mark. The ship now eased northbound, towards the same dock it departed from. Exactly six hundred feet from the dock entrance, Kathy waited, and leaned over, peering down into the water, as if the scooters would somehow magically surface. As the ship approached, an armed official holding a clipboard flew up the ramp in a motorcycle. When the vessel was secured, Scott waited alongside Mark for the captain. Mark's aunt waved up at him, and the gangway began its descent.

"You wait here," said the captain, as he walked down the ramp towards the official, and handed him an envelope. After conversing for a minute, the captain walked back up onto the ship.

"Okay Mark, you're good to go."

Scott followed Mark down to the dock to greet Kathy. After Mark got his obligatory hugs, Scott introduced himself.

"Hi, I'm Scott Kobara. You must be Kathy."

"Yes. I'm honored to meet you."

"My pleasure. Mark speaks kindly of you. I do find it interesting that he was able to find his way down here and board our ship."

"That was all me," said Kathy. "I was responsible for planning the whole thing. I talked him into it. If you want to press charges, I did it."

"Well quite the contrary. You see, Mark getting on the ship was a win-win situation. If it went along without a hitch, he would have gotten to play against some of the best players from Europe. But the air conditioning problem opened up a different door for Mark."

"What's that?" asked Kathy.

"About thirty five miles from New York City, I own a house in Armonk, and my table tennis club is in nearby Hawthorne. Koji Yamaguchi, along with his wife and daughter live in Hawthorne. Occasionally, their guests, or mine, stay for extended periods of time. Both of them are excellent cooks, and love to entertain. Of course there are two ping pong tables downstairs in the humungous basement, which is dug out and sports a ten foot ceiling. The Metro train to Manhattan is just minutes away."

"Sounds like a fantastic place," said Kathy.

"Well you, and of course the young star here, are welcome to stay for as long as you like. Koji is a superb coach, and would greatly look forward to working with such a talented young gentleman. You don't have to decide immediately though. I'll be cruising and schmoozing with the Europeans, and getting my butt kicked on the tables."

"Koji Yamaguchi. He's a legend," said Mark.

"Mark will get to spend a lot of time sparring with Koji, and with some of the best in the world at the club."

"I'm not sure I can afford to spend much time in such an expensive area," replied Kathy.

"Look. I will make sure that you have the resources to enjoy your stay. Consider this an investment in Mark."

Kathy looked at Mark, and his eyes said it all. She nodded to Scott, and a group hug ensued, enveloping Scott.

"Fantastic. Here, I'll text you the address, and their information. I will give the Yamaguchi's a heads up, and you let them know specifically when you expect to arrive. Mark, work hard with Mr. Yamaguchi, and Kathy, you enjoy yourself."

"I can stay for a bit," said Kathy. "I guess I planned to be away for a while anyway."

"Should I tell mom and dad?" asked Mark.

"Your dad would be out of his mind about it, and that would

put a damper on the whole thing. Let's see what it's all about and enjoy it for a bit, then we can decide. It's not as crazy as sneaking onto the ship, you know."

Out of earshot, Scott took out his cell and called Koji.

"Hey guy. You won't believe this one. On the way to netting the big whale, I snagged a trophy fish, a wannabe stowaway looking to show off his talents. His name is Mark Linderman. Sixteen he is, self-trained, raw, and powerful. He cut through Skip like butter, and I think his upside is huge. The ship had a little problem so it will be a week late getting to Lisbon. It's back in Florida now for a short repair. I offered up your house and services. Believe me, this is so bizarre, this kid is really special, and he is self-motivated. His aunt will be coming along. They will probably arrive in a couple days."

"I can't wait to hear about all the details. No problem. We'll get things ready," replied Koji.

The *Uber* driver was kind enough to stop at a mom and pop drive up where Kathy popped for extra-large, extra thick chocolate shakes. Extracting the globs from the concrete mixers proved to be laborious, but extremely satisfying. Twenty minutes ticked off the westbound hop across the southern peninsula before the first sip turned into the first slurp. In another forty, the satisfied duo arrived home. Kathy booked a flight for the day after tomorrow and exchanged texts with Koji. She scurried about, doing laundry and getting packed. Tomorrow would just be a down day, a day to enjoy the pool, and the comforts of home.

CHAPTER 8

THE GIRL

The non-stop 737 banked to the left in its final approach to LaGuardia. Mark relished the window seat, awestruck by the magnificent skyline. Next to him, Kathy craned to catch the last of the stunning views before touchdown. Her past trips had familiarized her with the transit system, and after a shuttle ride, they climbed on the North Metro Line train. Brick structures straddling the tracks, and the terrain gradually transitioned to green and open spaces. The train braked again as the duo hung on in the vestibule. Signs above the platform confirmed they had arrived at Hawthorne, and they exited the sliding doors. A short walk to the parking lot revealed a man standing in front of his brown full-sized sedan. Above his dark shorts, his arms were folded across his bright red shirt.

"That's him," said Mark.

As they approached him, he extended his arms outward.

"Koji?" asked Kathy.

"Welcome to Hawthorne. Welcome to New York," he called out, smiling.

The fit and youthful appearing father subtly bowed, and extended his hand to greet Kathy with a gentle handshake. A ten-fold increase in clamping power awaited Mark's outstretched paw as the two locked eyes.

"C'mon, let me put your things in the trunk, and let's go meet my wife, and maybe my daughter is home now."

The suburban brick and sided two-story home was set back a hundred and fifty feet from the road. Bounded on each side by mature maple trees, the structure was generously separated from the neighbors on both sides. Short of the garage, Koji pulled right next to the side entrance, and stopped underneath the carport. He began with a brief history as they stepped out of his sedan.

"This is where Scott lived for most of his childhood, and he wanted to hang on to the property after he moved. He didn't want to risk renting the property to just anyone, so he lets us stay here— no strings attached. We've been friends for a long time, and I frequently help him out at his club. We expanded the upstairs, and occasionally he will have his guests stay here, like you guys. His house is about five miles from here, in a beautiful area."

"It's very lovely here," said Kathy.

From underneath the carport, the two guests and Koji filed through the mudroom and into the kitchen. The windows were wide open on this mild June afternoon, yet an amazing aroma stayed imprisoned.

"This is my wife Kate, and my daughter Leah."

Leah took a couple of short steps and maneuvered in front of Mark. Halfway between her black Converse low tops and obsidian hued strands, her palm emerged. The soft handshake completed the spell her eyes had started.

"Dad says you're awesome!" she blurted, jolting Mark out of his daze.

"Ah, I've never won anything."

Kate quickly stepped forward to meet Kathy and spoke.

"Let me show you the upstairs. You can figure out which rooms you want. Oh, your packages arrived in good shape, and you have about a half hour to settle in before dinner. I left the router passcode on a sticky note in each room, along with all our cell numbers."

The upstairs was composed of four modest bedrooms, two baths, and a small all purpose room containing a counter, sink, large table, and mini refrigerator. Some of Leah's artwork sat on the table in the bright studio-like area, surrounded by windows on three sides. Leah's bedroom had an outside entrance extending out to a small deck, with stairs leading down to the expansive unfenced backyard. The mature and trusted daughter was the gatekeeper of the upstairs.

"Dinner," called Kate.

Kathy and Mark sat across from the Yamaguchi's at the thick, rough-hewn, shellacked table. A steaming casserole sat squarely in the middle, as flames from two candles danced on each end.

"Yum." Kathy said. "This is excellent. What's in it?"

"Well, it's got Maine Lobsters, crackers, cream, pretty much the kitchen sink after that."

Leah woofed down her dinner, and signaled to Mark as he polished off his last bite.

"Come on downstairs."

"We'll be down in a while," said Koji.

"Leah seems so intelligent and composed," said Kathy.

"Somehow she gained wisdom beyond her seventeen years," said Koji. Mark seems like a sharp kid."

"For sure. He's a bit behind when it comes to *life's experiences*. That's all," said Kathy. "This little excursion is certainly a jump start though."

Leah and Mark descended down a lengthy flight of concrete stairs. Leah flipped the lights and the cavernous room came alive.

"Wow!" exclaimed Mark.

The ten foot ceiling was cathedral-like for a basement. Sturdy round pillars supported an oversized I-beam, which split the subterranean playground. A set-up ping pong table occupied the barren left side as one entered. A stroll over to right side, revealed a pinball machine, flat screen TV, sofa, and refrigerator. In the far corner sat a second ping pong table, folded up like a pair of butterfly wings. A well-populated trophy case shimmered with gold.

"Are all those your Dad's?" asked Mark

"Well, there's a sprinkling of mine in there."

"You played?"

"Dad got me into it for a while, but he decided it would be best for me if I tried a variety of activities. Most of my trophies in there are from when I was really young, and a couple are from other sports."

Mark walked over to the case bending to read the engravings.

"That's you, first place in the U1500…and there it is, your dad's second place in the World Championships in 1997, along with the paddle he used. He should have won. There's one with a win last year in the Over 40 division."

'Chalk up' echoed from the corner of the room as Leah's arms straddled the sides of *Eight Ball Deluxe*. She retracted the plunger and fired the silver ball into play. With each flip, her body contorted as if she stepped on an ant colony. Although she tried to be in control, the stationary machine seemed to dictate her movements. The sounds, flashing lights, and body language again had Mark spellbound.

"Your turn. It's 1980's technology, but it's my favorite pinball of all time," she said, taking Mark from his hypnotic state.

The pair traded places back and forth for fifteen minutes when the adults appeared.

"I've got the next two days off, so Mark and I are taking the train downtown," said Leah, with this being news to Mark as well.

Everyone remained downstairs until well into the evening with the visitors heading up to finishing unpacking, and turn in after a day of travel. The teens slept in, and Leah wanted to wait until rush hour was over to head out anyway. After a couple bowls of cereal, they began their walk to the station.

"Are you sure your dad doesn't want me to practice today?"

"It's just one day."

I don't have that much money with me," said Mark humbly.

"Don't worry. I've got a couple part time jobs this summer. Ever since I got the full ride to Cornell, Dad's wallet is halfway out of his back pocket whenever I look at him. I know, nobody likes to be a sponge, but you didn't expect to be here. The city can be very expensive, but there's a lot of stuff we can see that is free."

"Cornell. I've heard of it"

"It's only about three hours from here. Dad wanted me to stay close."

"Where do you work?"

"I work three mornings at a small electronics company in the next suburb over and test circuit boards. One day a week I work in an art supply store, just because I like it."

"I saw some drawings in the basement and upstairs. Did you do those?"

"Yeah."

"Nice."

As the Metro North Line pulled into Grand Central Terminal Leah turned to Mark.

"Let's go to the top of the Empire State Building. We can walk to it. It's less than a mile. It costs, but it's super worth it. After that, we'll just spend money on transportation and some food."

When the elevator doors opened, Leah grabbed Mark's hand and led him over to the fencing surrounding the 86th floor observation deck. It was quite clear, and not crowded yet.

"Take some pictures," said Leah.

"Whoa, let me get used to this for a minute."

As the pair circumnavigated the open air deck, Leah pointed to some of the famous landmarks on each side.

"See, the Statue of Liberty, The Brooklyn Bridge."

After a half hour, the pair were zipped to ground level and walked over to Times Square.

"This is it, Broadway, the theater district, Times Square, you know, New Year's Eve. You have to see it at night sometime. Let's hit Central Park," said Leah, immediately flagging a cab.

"The Dakota," Leah told the driver who immediately floored it, channeling his inner NASCAR self. She jokingly put her hands over Mark's eyes. "It's best not to watch sometimes."

The vehicle zoomed and weaved northbound to the Upper West Side, dropping them in front of the famous apartment building. Across the street, Leah purchased two hot dogs and a large drink from a street vendor. Sitting on a wall next to Strawberry Fields, She stuck two straws into the cup.

"What's in the park?" asked Mark.

"There's a zoo, conservatory, lakes, boats, stages, trails, museums, baseball fields. Too much to see in a day. Let's just walk up to the small castle, and then back down what they call the Mall. Then we can take a short subway ride back down to Grand Central."

Returning from the serene canopy of overhanging trees, the pair transitioned underground to the noise and bustle of the subway.

"That's ours, said Leah. Stay right next to me, and hold on. You may have to push your way through people when it's time to exit, but that's expected. Nobody takes it personal."

Leah texted her mom when they got on the Metro and then turned to Mark.

"It's barbeque tonight at the house. Tomorrow—I'll ask this time. How would you like to take a ride to Cornell? It's right next to one of the Finger Lakes. We have to leave early."

"Are you sure it's okay with your dad?"

"My dad's cool. He'll do anything for me."

The Yamaguchi family and the two guests gathered at the table on the patio for some slow cooked pork, mashed potatoes, and beans. Koji had been at the club for part of the day, but table tennis didn't dominate the conversation. Kathy was going to go downtown tomorrow, so Leah recapped what her and Mark did. The teens finished up and Leah grabbed a couple bikes from the garage. Her and Mark rode around the neighborhoods, and then picked up a couple of cones in town, as dusk came upon them.

The next morning, Kate was up before everyone, and threw a couple tuna sandwiches, munchies, and Cokes into a cooler. When Mark and Leah came downstairs, two steaming bowls of oatmeal sat atop the island. The teens polished off their breakfast, and slipped into Kate's small SUV, exactly at 7:30.

"Do you drive?" asked Leah.

"I got my license, but I'm kind of a bike person."

"Me too. I've only driven up there once before out of the three times I have visited Cornell."

"What's your major?"

"Some kind of Engineering, maybe environmental."

"Cool."

Leah's driving mirrored her calm and self-assured personality. Mark was intoxicated by this maturity, something he never experienced in Montana. Sure, there were girls there who were secretly interested in him, but they couldn't display it, the jocks ruled.

"Do you want me to turn the air conditioning on?" asked Leah.

"No!" Mark said spontaneously. "I mean, if you want to, that's okay."

Leah cracked the windows and tuned the radio to an *eighties through today* format, just audible over the road noise. It didn't override the conversation, until Taylor Swift came on, when Leah tacked on a few decibels, getting a nod from Mark.

"What was your high school like?" asked Mark.

"Oh, Hawthorne, I loved it, and did a lot of activities. You don't feel pressured to get into anything. There's arties, brains, nerds, jocks, freaks. You know, the usual groups. I stayed away from the cliques, and always felt safe there."

The pair pulled into the parking lot, and approached the McGraw Clock Tower. High atop the tower, chimes echoed over the campus.

"Let's go," said Leah.

The pair raced up the stairs, all one hundred sixty-one of them. Mark led until he purposely tripped on the last few stairs.

"Dead heat," he said.

Pausing to catch their breath, they took in the birds-eye viewpoint of the picturesque campus.

"I'm winded," said Leah.

"Me too."

"There's the engineering quad and the Cascadilla Gorge Trail. Let's check out the quad, and then hike the trail," suggested Leah.

Signs along the gorge warned visitors to stay on the restored path. The cliffs, waterfalls, rushing water, and deep pools were as deadly as they were beautiful. Underneath the tree canopies, railings separated hikers from the slippery shale. Steep stairs led Mark and Leah up and out of the gorge.

"Awesome. I'm hungry," said Mark.

"Me too. Let's eat by the lake, and then head over to the falls," said Leah taking the soft pack out of the trunk.

Nestled in just north of the campus, the serene Lake Beebe could melt away many stresses, including those of finals week. The trees outlining the lake were reflected in the calm waters, and would dazzle in the fall, portending the snowy winter. Two paddles rippled the glassy surface as a couple guided their canoe towards the shore. Presumably, slinging his paddle around the Florida clubs was supposed to ease Mark's frustrations. Now, without lifting a finger, his acrimony slowly evaporated into the upstate New York sky.

CHAPTER 9

THE ZEN MASTER

Koji was quite smitten with the way Leah had taken to Mark, and neither parent was getting in the way of things. Even if Mark stuck around, this couldn't turn into an extended bash before Leah went off to school. Scott was driven, he needed results fast. But Koji allowed a couple days for things to percolate before he had to get down to business. Mark was just fine in the Yamaguchi's book. He was polite, nice looking, and well spoken. Not only did he have a common interest with Koji, but he packed a boatload of potential. Like clockwork, while Mark and Leah were on their way back from Cornell, Koji received a text from Scott.

Hey Koji, how are things going? I wanted to know your first impressions of the Mark's game, his strengths and weaknesses.

Scott, things have been busy around here with Mark getting settled, and I need a little more time to work with him and to give you a detailed evaluation.

No problem, replied Scott.

Scott was certainly not sending Mark to Hawthorne for a paid vacation, and definitely would have been peeved knowing a couple days were frittered away without any training. Koji repeatedly glanced out the front window, and finally at 5:30 Leah pulled into the driveway.

"Did you guys have fun?" asked Koji as they walked inside.

"Yeah," the pair answered in unison.

"It's a beautiful setting up there," added Koji. "You know Scott texted me today and wanted to know how we were smacking the balls around. Why don't you change and we can get an hour in before dinner."

Koji went downstairs, wiped off the table, and swept the floor that surrounded the playing area. He was in the midst of some stretching exercises when Mark and Leah came down. Koji was in impeccable condition for forty two. He was still a 2450 rated player, quite amazing for someone who didn't play much anymore. In fact, he was in the upper tier of players in the United States over the age of forty. The matching black shorts and top with diagonal red blazes justified his authenticity. Mark's clothes could hardly have been more wrinkled.

Not only was Mark standing across from someone that had taken the top Chinese player to the brink, but Leah pulled up a stool off to the side. When Mark unexpectedly surprised Scott and Skip on the ship, he was still carrying his Montana edge with him. The kids at school, the social media postings, and his dad. They all drove him, and were a part of every shot. His debut aboard The Ping was still laced with that venom. In a couple days, the tranquilizing effect of Leah's presence had extracted much of that out of him.

Mark and Koji began warming up with the obligatory forehand to forehand volleys, which in seconds, transitioned from a school zone pace, to the Autobahn. They switched to the backhand, then chop to chop, block to block, loop to loop before playing some mock points without keeping score. Koji subtly toned his shots down, to avoid demoralizing Mark. Scott was a keen judge of talent, and there was no way he was going to send someone pedestrian to Koji. Koji sensed something had to be wrong. Mark's eyes lacked fire. For the next half hour, the two went through the motions of high level play, which certainly would have dazzled most. A tenacity was lacking in Mark's efforts. Koji was giving him opportunities to take charge, but Mark only took a reactive stance.

"Okay, let's wrap it up for now," said Koji.

"I think I'm a little rusty," replied Mark, as he headed upstairs.

Koji signaled to Leah to stick around downstairs.

"What makes Mark tick?" asked Koji.

"What do you mean Dad?"

Well, you've been with him for a couple days. What does he like?"

"Obviously, he is obsessed with table tennis, and he really likes biking and hiking. He told me about his garage, and showed me the pictures on his tablet. He has all kinds of notes about the physics of table tennis. Since he was getting judged at school, he hardly looks at social media."

"If you want Mark to be around here for a while, you need to work with me. Tell me about his pictures, and just find out what you can. What time are you off work tomorrow?"

"I'm only working until one. I'll see what I can come up with."

"Head right home when you are off. I am going to have someone else help out at the club tomorrow evening."

"Sure Dad."

After dinner, while Leah and Mark were out for a bike ride, Koji approached Kathy.

"Hi Kathy, I need a little favor. Can you take Mark out tomorrow afternoon for some shopping and an early dinner?"

"Yeah, it's not like we have anything pressing. What's up?"

"We're just going to make some changes downstairs, but don't mention anything to him. If he gets back around six, that's fine."

"While Mark and Leah aren't around, I need to get something off my shoulders. Kate should be in this also. Said Kathy."

"I'll get her."

"There is something you should know, and it's getting deeper," said Kathy relaying the chain of events that occurred over the last week. "Mark's parents are completely in the dark, and sooner or later they will find out. I don't have a land line at home, so I have been able to use my cell to deceive them. They will likely insist Mark comes home, possibly take legal action, and probably never have anything to do with me."

"Hmm," said Koji. "Now a few more people would be disappointed if he had to go. I can understand Mark's parents being livid, and I can certainly understand Mark's passion for the game. I will suggest that Mark call his parents and explain what happened, and what he would like to do. He is far from any danger now, and I would like to say he is in very good hands."

When Leah arrived home at 1:30 the next day, the upstairs was empty, but repetitive pounding emanated from the basement. As she descended to check it out, four light green king size bed sheets were spread around the basement floor. Next to the ping pong table was a fifteen hundred watt space heater, two clamp lights, and some extension cords.

"Let's get busy," said Koji. "In that box there are six non-toxic spray cans and a smaller box of fabric markers. Just do things sketchy, we don't have a lot of time. Oh, and I'd wear that mask just to be safe,"

Leah began to outline her and her dad's ideas onto the first nine foot square sheet. She kept her work coarse, but recognizable. In ninety minutes her first piece took shape, a gorge, with overhanging trees and rushing water graced the canvas.

"What do you think Dad?"

"You are really super."

"Oh, and by the way. What was that *awesome* thing that came out of your mouth when you met Mark? That was completely out of character."

"I don't know. It just came out."

Koji climbed a ladder, and stapled the top of the first sheet to a ten foot long stud secured to the ceiling. Leah began sketching six unrecognizable faces across the second sheet. These were Mark's biggest high school detractors. In the same manner this mural was hung on the opposite side of the table, about eight feet away. The end sheets remained blank, hanging near the front and back walls of the basement, sixteen feet removed from the ends of the table.

Koji centered the two utility lights six feet above the table and plugged them into the extension cord. Heat began to radiate from the aluminum reflectors. Underneath, the space heater glowed, and spilled out warmth from the sides of the playing surface.

"Okay, Leah, grab that laundry basket over there and put it in the far corner, just for effect."

Koji ran upstairs and changed into a drab gray t-shirt and matching shorts, both in need of ironing. He found an old tattered white headband and stretched it over his forehead. As he returned to the basement, Leah burst out laughing when she saw him.

"He should be home in about a half hour," said Koji.

"I think I just heard mom come in. Hey Mom, c'mon down and check it out," called Leah.

"You guys—very clever. I hope he takes it well. I grabbed a few sandwiches for us to eat before they get back."

Koji and went back downstairs and right on schedule, Kathy, and Mark walked in carrying a couple of small shopping bags. Kate and Leah greeted them.

"Hi, did you guys have fun?" asked Kate.

"Yeah. We went to White Plains. I picked up a couple of

summer tops on clearance. Mark got some long pants. Then we slipped into a small Italian restaurant before five, and got the early special," replied Kathy.

"Koji is looking forward to you seeing you downstairs. So change into your new gear if you want, and head down."

Kate signaled to go downstairs, and in the dimness, behind the furthest sheet, they waited. Mark proceeded down the solid concrete steps, and flipped the light switch twice with no result. The glow of the heating coils drew him into the balmy playing area. Simultaneously, the two lights above him illuminated, and the small group emerged.

"Surprise," rang out in unison.

"We couldn't transport your garage two thousand miles," joked Koji, as Mark grappled for words. "And nobody here wants to see you back in there anytime soon."

The reality flash of a ticket home hit Mark instantly. If he didn't live up to expectations, it would be life back at the real garage, and everything that came with it. Leah was fine with Mark the way he was, but if she had to immerse herself in quirky motivations to keep him there, she would do what she needed. A geographic split between them was looming, but there was still six weeks left in summer.

Koji's apparel made it difficult to see a serious side of him, but he rested two palms on the table and leaned in towards Mark.

"Let me get philosophical. The faces on the sheet represent those who have scorned your passion, but your passion has opened up a new world for you. I want you to transition away from the negative energy that propelled you. Grow away from the anger that drove you. Look for new positive motivations."

"The sheet with the gorge has water, trees, and shale, representing calm, growth, and change. So stay calm under pressure, grow your mental and physical game, and adapt your tactics as needed. This is a good place to be. A place to stay smooth and calm.

"Your parents are with you at all times, in spirit. Leah's artwork is around us, and we are here for you—so let's lighten up dude, and smack some balls around. I really want to see what you've got."

The sheets straddled the table like security blankets. Mark was surrounded by people who cared. The morsels of animosity in his gut melted. He would have to draw from new and positive sources. As Koji put the first ball in play, a looseness and freedom came back to Mark's strokes. There was no score keeping, but the sixteen year old was keeping the 1990's American champion on his toes. With a fully drenched headband, Koji set his paddle on the table.

"We've put a solid hour in, and tomorrow will be a full day down here, so let's call it."

After the pair took their showers, Mark settled into the family room to play some video games with Leah, and Koji settled nestled up to the kitchen counter with his phone.

Scott. Sorry for the delay. Here's the update on Mark. First I made some changes to the playing environment. This seemed to help him relax, but over time as he gets comfortable I will need to wean him off of this setup. You are indeed still a great evaluator of talent, and if he doesn't get distracted, he is a keeper. He is smooth with cat-like reflexes and employs a variety of styles as needed. Since he has not been facing humans, I will concentrate mostly on strategy. Especially when to take advantage of opportunities, and when to wait. Also, where to serve, and how to handle different styles of service. We can develop these things, no problem.

Thanks guy. We're just about to Lisbon. Keep me posted. I will let you know how it is going here. Scott.

The next morning Kate made omelets for everyone, and Leah headed off to work. Koji and Mark finished eating, and before their first full day of training Koji addressed Mark.

"Before we start today, you need to call your parents. We really need permission from them to continue this. I don't envy you having to make the call, but it is right, and necessary."

"My dad will be very angry. I know I'll have to come home."

"Talk to your mom first, if possible. It's 7:00 out there now.

"My dad's probably left for work already, and my mom doesn't leave until eight."

"Great. Do it upstairs."

Mark picked up his phone. Tapping the home number awaited like the stinger of a yellow jacket, but he gingerly touched it, just enough to make the connection. The earliness of the call was disconcerting to Candice, but she answered in her usual chipper fashion.

"Hi Mark, you're calling early today."

"Yeah Mom. I'm fine. Don't worry. You know that Scott Kobara table tennis cruise—."

From there, Mark began to recount the events leading up to where he was now, and he continued.

"Yeah, the Yamaguchi's are so nice. Koji was almost a world champion, and he is so smart. And their daughter, Leah; we went to Manhattan, and then up to see her university.

"Do you like her?"

"I really like her. I don't know how long Kathy is going to stay, but instead of going back with her, can I spend the rest of the summer here?"

"Your dad and I are going to have to talk about it. You know he is not going to be happy."

"I know."

Before heading downstairs, Mark stretched out on his bed with his hands behind his head, staring at the ceiling for a couple minutes. Next, he was going to have to tell Kathy that Candice, and soon Carl would know.

"How did it go?" asked Koji.

"She mostly listened. Her and her sister used to do adventurous things, and my dad said they nearly died because of my aunt. He was dating my mom at the time and was really stressed out."

"I see. Let's go down and get some work in, I mean fun," said Koji.

Koji was not only masterful at the game, but his teaching methods were innovative and full of variety. Like the monologue of a late night talk show host, he attempted to keep it light and fresh every day. He would join Mark in the stretching and aerobics routine before engaging in the intensive drills. Simultaneously Koji would hit balls to Mark from one side of the table while a robot would intermittently expel the plastic projectiles from the other.

"Footwork, footwork," Koji repeated as Mark oscillated between forehand and backhand shots.

There was no good time for Candice to break the news to Carl, so she faced it head on, Minutes after he walked inside the door from work, she began.

"Mark called this morning."

"Yeah."

"He's fine, and he's happy."

"How's the pong down there?"

"He's actually playing in a different location. He and Kathy ended up on that table tennis cruise—and now they are in New York."

"I told you. It didn't take any time at all for her to go on a wild escapade. Go on."

They both sat down at the kitchen table, and after Candice finished with the details, Carl pounded his fist on the table.

"So she wasn't going to tell us that they would be on a ship for six weeks, and then she left him on it alone. That should be good for a couple years in jail."

"Security didn't have her arrested, so there's no record of it."

"I shouldn't be angry. This is my fault. It was a bad idea to let him go. Tell him to get his butt home. Now I can tell you my news. One quarter of the plant is being laid off, and I am one of them."

"Oh no. When?"

"Immediately. So you better get something more than that part-time school aide. There's not a lot around here, and now there's going to be more people looking for work."

"When it rains it pours. There's more to this Mark situation. He asked if he could stay at the family's house in New York since he was going to be away for two months anyway."

"We don't know anything about these people, and he's not a big city kid, c'mon."

"I guess the dad is a big time coach, and Mark has a thing for the daughter."

"In a couple days?"

"I really hate to say this, but if we make him come home, he's going to know you're the one who is behind it. It won't be good between you two. You could lose him for a long time."

"Thank you to your sister. Thank her very much for presenting me with these options. Going along with this, or having him angry at me for the rest of my life. What's your take?"

"Well, he could come home a much happier kid in six weeks. Just think of it as a taste of when he's away at college."

"Wow. What a day. You handle it. Find out what you can about that family. What's their name?"

"The Yamaguchi's."

"Asian?"

"Yeah."

Kate and Kathy spent the day in Manhattan, while Koji worked with Mark and slow cooked outside. Leah, her mom, and Kathy nearly walked in the door together, while the guys showered. It was a perfect evening, and the five ate at the picnic table on the patio.

"My mom called back today," said Mark, who waited until everyone was gathered to break the news. "She said I could stay here for the rest of the summer."

"That's fantastic news," said Kate.

"What did your dad say?" asked Koji.

"My mom said he just wanted me to be happy."

"You're welcome to stay here as well Kathy."

"I should really get back, and I miss my furry pal. Mark looks right at home already. I would just be a fifth wheel, so to speak."

"Not at all," added Koji.

That evening, Kathy booked a flight for the next day and called Candice.

"How mad is he?"

"You put him in quite a box, but I think it could work out okay."

"I hope I didn't put a huge strain on you guys."

"The strain was already here. Carl is laid off."

"No."

"Anyway. I sold Carl the long term picture. I said that Mark would be a happier person when he got back. What are the Yamaguchi's like? And what about that girl?"

"They're gold. The girl is mature beyond her years. That Scott guy, I just think he's just rich and eccentric. I don't think you have to worry about anything. So what are you guys going to do?"

"We might have to move to Billings. Carl is going to look. Things are booming there."

"Wow. At least Mark wouldn't have to return to Chinook. Just to let you know, they are very high on him here, and Scott can get pretty persuasive. I really never intended for things to get complicated."

"Don't worry. Some things needed to change anyway."

CHAPTER 10

THE ZENGMASTER

Approaching a billion and a half people, China has a huge pool of table tennis players to choose from. The Chinese flourish not only because of their sheer numbers, but the due to the intense training regimen, and the relative lack of distractions compared to Western and European nations. Seemingly born with a paddle in their hand, these diamonds in the rough, are whisked into the sport at an early age. Some top players fold under the pressure associated with the program, finding other avenues to pursue. That isn't a problem, there's another player right behind them, waiting in the wings.

Except for Leon Zeng. There was a chasm between him and his closest pursuers. He was swept into the program early, and rocketed up the ranks to become the men's champion at seventeen. He was a national hero, who would likely reign for years to come. At eighteen, the potential greatest player of all time abruptly walked away from the national team.

Living outside of Beijing, Leon settled for employment at a small factory, but those disappointed with him, constantly reminded him of it. So Leon disappeared into the countryside, changed his appearance, and found sanctuary with a small peasant family, who he helped in the fields. The poor community did have a ping pong table where Leon kept his talents under wraps, just playing to the level of the best village members.

The simple existence provided some short term relief for him, but he wanted a new life and applied for his passport. The reply was short, and unexpected. *Due to an unsettled civil matter, the application process for your passport has been delayed.* Leon knew of nothing, and months dragged on with no progress.

Underground smuggling operations were plentiful and generally reliable to those in the know. America was Leon's goal, but the going price was north of forty thousand dollars, and very risky. A portion could be paid once you were inside, but the gangs would be at your door if you went into arrears. With his cash savings, Leon dove into the underworld. He settled for Albania, hopefully an interim stop. Sandwiched beneath a false floor in a truck, he endured bouncy rides through poppy fields and other dangerous territories. His final stop of the harrowing trek, was in the capital city of Tirana.

Albania, like many European countries, was producing high level players. The Albanian Table Tennis Association was promoting play throughout the country, and the center of play was in Tirana. Table tennis was still in Leon's blood, but not the government sponsored hyper competitive kind. He avoided the clubs where the top players hung out, and opted for the low profile venues, like some of the back rooms behind store fronts. One of those existed in a restaurant where he gained employment doing prep work and washing dishes. Again, he curbed his unrivaled talents, stealthily tailoring his play to the level of his co-workers, and their friends.

Sporting spotty facial hair, tinted glasses, and often a knit cap, Leon kept his visibility low, sticking around the outskirts of town. He rented a room from an older woman, helped her with physical tasks, and often spent time with her grandson, who spoke fluent English.

Tirana is the largest city in the country with over 400,000 people, and the metropolitan area approaches twice that. It's big enough for someone to keep some anonymity. Although disputed, official statistics state that Albanians make up to ninety seven percent of the population. Not that your average citizen would recognize the ex-Chinese champ, but Leon represented a sliver of the population, and that garnered him the occasional double take.

One of the double takes came from Jeton Pojani, the owner of the largest table tennis club in Tirana. When he isn't playing or tending to the duties of the club, he is an avid cyclist, often tooling around the city and metro area, looking for new and obscure eateries.

Five years ago, at a tournament in Bratislava, Slovakia, sixteen year old Leon Zeng was in the final stages of his brilliant junior run. From there, he would begin his reign as the best player in the world. At the same event, an eleven year old was emerging onto the scene. The boy was none other than Jeton's son Lukas, the now current Albanian Junior champion. All the focus at the competition was on Zeng.

In the less trendy part of the city where Leon worked, Jeton was out on his bike, about four miles from his club. Zeng strolled along the sidewalk in the opposite direction.

"No way," said Jeton out loud, nearly brushing the cars on the right as he flashed back to the tournament.

Anyone who followed the international scene knew Leon had disappeared, but this was a longshot. By the time Jeton made it around the tightly parked cars to the sidewalk, Leon had stepped inside his restaurant, and disappeared into the back room. Jeton entered three successive store fronts, straining to get a look in the back, but saw nothing.

Jeton rode around to the back of the businesses. Clouded out windows sat well above eye level, and one back door sat ajar. Shelves full of boxes blocked his view inside, but the unmistakable sound of bouncing ping pong balls emanated outwards. Wary of looking suspicious, Jeton high-tailed it back to the club. As he pulled up some images, he gained more confidence that his suspicions were correct.

The following day, Jeton returned and sipped his coffee al fresco across the street. His vantage point would give him time to cross and intercept his target. On schedule, Leon came into view, and Jeton hastily abandoned his table, causing a car to stop abruptly.

"Leon!" He called, twenty feet removed from the restaurant.

"Sorry, my name is Li."

"Zeng that is," said Jeton authoritatively.

"I'm not who you're looking for. But if you think it's me, what do you want?"

"I want my son to get some coaching from you."

"I'd like to get to America."

"Look, I can contact the Chinese Embassy, or the local authorities."

"I am here legally."

"I doubt it, the way you hide your appearance and stick around here. I can have you checked out easily enough."

"Okay, okay. Please don't."

"Come over and sit with me across the street."

"I only have ten minutes."

A passing car nearly struck the pair as they returned to Jeton's table. Now sitting across from each other, Leon asked.

"Who are you?"

"Jeton. I own the big club in town. Do you remember playing my son Lukas in Bratislava?"

"No. I remember the tournament."

"I'd like you to coach my son."

"There's a lot of good coaches."

"There's only one greatest in the world."

"Not me anymore."

"So how do you think you're going to get into the United States?" asked Jeton.

"I'll have to establish citizenship somewhere, get a passport, a visa, or get help."

"Well if you coach my son, I could help you."

"Coach your son with just a promise, I don't know you. Remember, if you do expose me, I won't be around to coach. When you come up with something real, you know where to find me."

"Come by the club and play. I'll protect you."

"Don't count on it."

The two split from the table.

The fifty year anniversary of Ping Pong Diplomacy was approaching in two years. A half decade ago the U.S. team travelled to Beijing and a new era of relations began between the United States and China. Scott, in awe of this development, immersed himself in the details. In 1972, he attended the Friendship Games, held in Nassau County, New York. It was a marvelous event, but only one American was able to scrape up a victory against the mighty Chinese visitors. The young and broke college student would go on to fulfil his dreams of designing concert halls, but another seed was planted. He himself didn't have the tools, but he developed a deep desire to witness an American champion in his lifetime.

Anniversary celebrations of PPD over the years, had been tepid, in terms of competition. There were returning players, exhibition matches, and items of nostalgia. Recently, tensions were again heating up between the two countries, tariffs were multiplying. There were disputes on currencies, territories, pollution, and piracy. Diplomacy was needed. Scott Kobara began pounding the table for a full blown fiftieth anniversary of the watershed event. He now had the influence and connections to get this ball rolling.

The Ping was three days into the Mediterranean. All forty eight patrons were onboard, and engrossed in the unique venue. The high level of play extended into the wee hours. It wasn't just the European men that playfully toyed with Scott. A group of spouses and girlfriends had *game*, and a couple put Skip back on his heels, making for must watch matches. For those done for the evening, a late night chef provided fare for the night owls. Outside, a trio filled the evening air with smooth jazz. The sound of the bouncing balls, like music, provided the universal language spoken inside the great room.

Scott would be returning to Tirana where, three years ago he played in Jeton's aging table tennis club. Together, they scoped out a larger and newer warehouse. Private clubs were always a hit and miss operation, financially speaking, and If Scott did have one redeeming quality, it was promoting the game and helping it flourish. So as Scott had done in a few other countries, he divvyed out ideas and financial support to Jeton for his new endeavor.

As the new club continued to be viable, the pair periodically conversed. The appearance of Leon Zeng, spurred an immediate phone call from Jeton, Two days later, Scott concocted a plan, and the phone call was the genesis for the *The Ping of the Seas*. Leon wanted to come to America, and Scott wanted to pair him with Koji to form a dream coaching team. Jeton was not going to let Leon go to America without Lukas going along and getting this high level training. Jeton's poker chip was information, incriminating information. One phone call could take Scott and Leon down if Lukas was left behind. Scott knew this, it went unspoken. Lukas was a cost of doing business. So Scott arranged for Lukas to live and train at the Yamaguchi's, and attend Hawthorne High School as an exchange student. All parties were happy.

All Scott needed was a quintessential American born prospect he could put into the hands of his two master coaches. When he returned from the voyage, he intended on reinvigorating his search. But a rare bird from Montana fell out of the heavens, and onto the deck of The Ping, changing everything. A viable challenger to the Chinese in Ping Pong Diplomacy II had been merely *pie in the sky*, but now the ingredients were on terra firma.

Not only did Scott contribute to the club in Tirana, but after the news of Leon, he arranged indirect payments to a local craftsman. A gift of appreciation was being constructed by this skilled woodworker. Jeton doled out Scott's payments, and oversaw the progress of the project.

The traditional particle board, or fiberboard commonly used in the making of many ping pong tables, would have no place in this work. Scott wanted something that would dazzle onlookers and yet be functional. He insisted on imported *Celery Top Pine*. Sporting arched sides and smooth rolling state of the art casters, the piece was beautiful and functional. Curly maple outlined the gorgeous top which was sprayed with multiple coats of varnish.

The Ping of the Seas slowed as it approached the port of Durres, Albania. Scott chomped his gum incessantly, peering at the coastline. Unlike the Atlantic crossing, the ship was no longer Scott's personal water taxi. There were nearly a hundred people on board, and security at the dock was noticeably tighter. This was the stop, the destination where Scott's gift of appreciation, would be bestowed upon him. Buses waited to take the passengers into town. Some would hit the club in Tirana. The others would go into Durres for the morning, and then Tirana in the afternoon. There, all parties would reunite for an evening banquet.

As the ship docked, the passengers exited and gathered around the shrouded nine by five foot masterpiece. Scott descended down the ramp, with forty players from Jeton's club standing on the dock behind the gift. Holding a small megaphone, Jeton came to the forefront to speak. He raised his hand to command quiet and began the celebration.

"Mr. Kobara. You have been generous to us with your advice, and financial support. Our club is thriving, and on behalf of the members of the Tirana Table Tennis Club, we would like to present you with this gift of our appreciation. Skip, why don't you stand over here next to Scott, you have been instrumental as well."

Reaching over the table with both hands, Jeton whisked off the sheet.

"I don't know what to say," replied Scott as he walked completely around the table, sans the net. He brushed his palm over the smooth finish. "It's spectacular."

"We hope it has a special place in your club."

"Oh, no doubt. Thank you all so much," said Scott, exchanging handshakes with the attendees. Waving, and heading back towards the ship, Scott and Skip accompanied two workers as they rolled the *Trojan horse* into the cargo opening.

"I'll be right back out. I forgot something," yelled Scott.

The din from the ship may have overridden any cough or sneeze coming from the mouth of Leon Zeng, but he held a dense cloth to his face in the case of an emergency. At five foot eight and one hundred forty pounds, he stretched out flat and diagonally in the shallow hidden cavity. The foam which lined the compartment, provided some internal comfort and noise reduction. Numerous small holes allowed sufficient oxygen to enter, while a water bottle and energy bar filled Leon's oversized pockets.

"Where do you want it?" asked one of the workers.

"Put it on the freight elevator and let me think about it a minute." replied Scott.

As the workers remained in the cargo area Scott slid into the elevator and hit the seventh floor button. Skip returned to the where the buses were beginning to load, and spoke to a small gathering.

"Scott forgot something in his room, and I think nature called. He should be right back."

Inside the ship, the agonizingly slow elevator climb began.

"Okay Leon, let's go," exclaimed Scott authoritatively.

The sound of a sliding latch was followed by a thud, as the trap door struck the elevator floor. Leon Zeng slid out from underneath the table and reached back under to close the hatch. The pair stared at each other eye to eye, equally astonished, and they shook hands. When the elevator stopped, Scott flipped a switch holding the doors open and scanned the hallway. He motioned to Leon and quickly led him down the hall and into room 715.

"Lock the door, be quiet, and don't let anyone in. There's two sandwiches and a coke over there. We'll be back tonight," said Scott, gesturing and pointing with each instruction.

Scott quick stepped it back to the elevator, closed the doors, and descended. He hustled back down the ramp and scurried over to the buses. Climbing aboard winded, he offered up an excuse for his tardiness as the bus rumbled away.

"Sorry guys. I didn't have my paddle case with me—and nature called," he said, sucking wind.

Scott sat down next to Skip and gave him a nod. He pulled out his phone and sent a text to Koji,

The Zengmaster is secured.

The Ping cruised into the western portion of the Mediterranean, two days before the Europeans would depart from the first cruise of its kind. Meanwhile, a small pair of headphones streamed English into his brain for each day for hours. He was resolute in his quest for fluency.

CHAPTER 11

THE CHANGING OF THE GUARDIANSHIP

In Hawthorne, Mark remained steadfast in his commitment. He burned calories at a torrid pace, as Koji transitioned his diet to one of a Tour de France rider. In less than a month, Mark was beginning to show additional tone and definition. Koji was treating this regimen as if a long term commitment was imminent. After all, Mark was entrenched, and totally buying in. How could his parents whisk him away from this, and relegate him back to his recreational seclusion?

Mark's mom would move anywhere. She remained in Montana after meeting Carl at school. Carl was another story. Montana was his home, period. The clock was ticking for high school registration. Drawing from the self-assured nature of Leah, and her supporting father, Mark prepared to tackle his situation head on. Rather than using his mom as the conduit for softening up his dad, Mark readied himself for a confrontation, and called home.

"Hi Mark," answered Candice, holding her cordless phone.

"Is Dad there?"

"Yeah, hang on a minute."

"What's up son?"

"I want to stay here for the school year."

"Have you really thought it out?"

"I've been here a month, and everyone is so nice."

"If you got involved in other activities in Chinook, you would meet more people and find them nice as well. I know a lot of this is about pong, but realistically you are getting older, and the money you can make from it isn't worth the time invested."

"I have an idea for a sensor that can make a robot more intuitive. Leah is going to help me develop it."

"Mom and I will have to talk."

Mark turned the tables going to his dad first. The Yamaguchi's would have to comply with the demands of Mark's parents, even if Mark dug his heels in.

"So what do we do?" Asked Carl. "We are in the same boat as when he asked to stay for there for the summer. Now it could be a year, or two years. He will blame me if we decide he must come home, and if we have to sell the house and get an apartment, he will have no place to practice. Right now, my only job prospect is in Billings."

"I hear everything you are saying."

"Let's sleep on it, said Carl."

When Carl got up the next morning, he opened his e-mails.

Payment received.

"Hey Candice, check this out. Is this some kind of scam?"

Carl logged into his bank account and looked at his mortgage statement.

Zero Balance. You are released from further payment obligations.

"It looks official," said Candice. "A little gift from Kobara. He does throw money around to get what he wants. I think it's a message that he wants Mark to stay in New York. Maybe there *is* a payoff in ping pong."

"That's extremely generous on his part. Without the pressure of having to sell our house quickly, we can take our time looking around Billings, if I get that job."

"Are you okay with Mark living in Hawthorne for at least for the next two years?"

"I have to respect his wishes and happiness, and it seems like the best outcome, as long as you are totally comfortable with the family. It's like he is away at college, but I was totally unprepared for this, it happened so fast."

"I know. Don't worry, I know this isn't worth much to you, but Kathy says the Yamaguchi's are wonderful. Their daughter, like Mark, is a straight A and above student. I'll go out there and meet them if it's awkward timing with your job prospect. If anything looks fishy, we can scrap the whole idea. I'll talk to our attorney, and make sure this can be handled in your absence, and that we are able to back out of it anytime."

"I trust your instincts."

"I'll call the Yamaguchi's and talk to Mark. That will start the ball rolling."

For over an hour in the Yamaguchi's kitchen, the cordless phone was passed around from Koji to Kate, and Mark to Leah. On the other end of the line, in Big Sky Country, the apprehensions of Mark's parents melted away with each minute. Warmth radiated from the handsets at both ends, and a verbal agreement was reached. Never in the conversation did it come up, that soon an undocumented person would be living in the household; a person who would be spending hours upon hours directly training Mark. Koji called Scott, and the legal wheels would begin to turn. Scott knew the local attorneys, and how to get things expedited.

As far as the court was also concerned, the only other guest coming to the Yamaguchi's was Lukas, the sixteen year old exchange student from Albania. Jeton and Lukas had no clue that the fastest rising star in the United States would be residing in the household. Scott was in no hurry to leak this out before he secured Leon. He didn't need a deal breaker before Leon was securely inside the Yamaguchi's premises. Scott was now completely absorbed in the development of Mark. Snagging this one of a kind kid from Montana was the mother of all unintended consequences. A perfect storm on calm seas.

The Yamaguchi's and Mark picked up Candice from LaGuardia and headed back to the Hawthorne residence. The house was nearly always perfect, but Kate did a little extra staging for this special guest. Scott stopped over, and Kate and Koji killed it again with their cooking skills.

Privately, in the backyard, Candice engaged Scott.

"Look, Carl and I cannot thank you enough for your extreme generosity and the way you have helped Mark expand his horizons."

"Oh, I enjoy helping people. Mark is one of a kind. I could see it immediately."

The next day, in front of a judge in White Plains, the Yamaguchi's were granted physical guardianship of Mark. The Lindermans would retain legal custody of Mark, and hold onto essentially all the rights parents normally have. Carl was in Billings, and able to handle his legal end of things in absentia.

The beautiful and growing city of Billings is home to one hundred and seventy five thousand residents. The Lindermans would now find themselves in this Gateway to Yellowstone Park. Job opportunities were sprouting up, and Carl was able to snag one of these in the commercial refrigeration business. They would be six hours from Chinook, and only twenty minutes to Billings Logan International. Leon would be arriving at the Yamaguchi's soon, and Lukas shortly thereafter. Leah would be leaving for Cornell in the middle of August. Mark and Lukas would attend Hawthorne High School as juniors. Changes for everyone.

For a player to become the top player, he has to train with the best. With a ranking of 3175 at his peak, Leon Zeng was the best, with room to spare. Having him as a sparring partner, was a sure ticket to improvement. He was the ultimate measuring stick, the bar to hurdle. If you could give him a game, you were world class. Although he was a few years removed from his top ranking, he kept his game simmering, and remained in excellent condition.

Koji was almost the best once, and now brought other things to the table. Some were intangibles and some were props. Psychology, strategy, motivation, and humor were sprinkled into his training mix. Now he had Mark to work with, a home baked cookie still on the rise, clumpy, with prime ingredients, but unevenly cooked. Mark's game had too much variety for any cookie cutter type approach. Koji was ideal.

Lukas was the typical table tennis prodigy. Before he could comfortably see over the table in his basement, he would stand on a modified pallet and hit balls back to his dad. When he was eight, his dad bought a dilapidated building and started his own club. Volunteers armed with rags and paint helped make it a respectable place to play. Jeton kept a workshop in the back of the facility, and made specialized tools for customers. Lukas essentially lived at the club. He would do his homework there after school, and stay all day when school wasn't in session. He'd find other members to play when his dad was busy, or hit against the robot. The father-son combo would close the place down late into the evening. Inside Albania, Lukas won nearly every tournament he played in.

That kind of commitment was difficult in the United States. How much of a normal American life could a teen be permitted to live, and still present a challenge to the top players in the world? This was where Koji was going to have to excel. Mark's life had been anything but normal. He essentially lived in his garage, devoid of the outside world. That all changed over the last month, and Leah entered the equation. The looming diversions awaited Lukas, including the short train ride to the *Big Apple*. Training the teens, managing the distractions, and keeping Mr. Zeng under wraps, were all squarely piling up on the Yamaguchi's plate.

CHAPTER 12

THE ARRIVAL

No one had ever gone to these great lengths to secure a table tennis player, and Scott was entering the most critical phase of this operation. Leon would not last long housed in a small compartment in the middle of a Miami summer. Any delays in disembarking could be deadly. Skip arranged for a refrigerated box truck to be delivered to the parking lot leading to the dock. The custom table resided in the great room and had been used by players sparingly. With a springy surface, it turned out to be more of a novelty item.

As the ship docked, Skip headed down the ramp and began his walk down the long dock to the parking lot. Unexpectedly, an armed security guard with a German Shephard was posted at the bow of the ship. Skip nearly stopped in his tracks upon seeing the dog, before returning to a normal gait.

"I'll be back with a truck," Skip told the guard after showing his papers.

Skip immediately texted Scott when he climbed in the truck,

There's an armed security guard with a German Shephard on the dock at the front of the ship. He's not the guy that was there when we returned for the repairs. I really hope your theory works. I mean, I am right there if we get caught.

I planned for it, but didn't really expect it. I'll take the fall. You had no idea that there was anyone in that compartment. Trust me. Replied Scott.

Scott's choice of wood for the table needed to meet four different criteria. Celery Top Pine met all of them. It was strong, beautiful, easy to work with, and most importantly aromatic. Scott only theorized it would mask the human scent, and it would take little time for sweat to develop in the Miami heat. Much of the table was coated with polyurethane, but the interior compartment was unfinished. Scott dashed over to a small tool case and pulled out a coarse sheet of sandpaper. He climbed underneath and began roughing up the interior cavity, and then spots around the perimeter of the playing surface, generalizing the scent.

He pushed the table from the great room and rolled it onto the freight elevator. Leon continued to endure the torture of sitting in a tub of cold water. Scott froze the elevator doors open and ran over to Leon's room.

"Okay. Dry off just enough so you don't drip, and do it quickly!"

Donning only a pair of swim trunks, Leon grabbed a towel and hastily got the bulk of the water off his body. He held an ice cold rag to his forehead. It would help muffle a sneeze or cough, but not enough to elude the keen ears of a trained dog.

Scott handed Leon a dust mask.

"Put this on. There's going to be a dog sniffing around the table, so it is extremely important that you remain perfectly still. If the scent of the wood does its job, we will have completed the most difficult step of the journey."

Leon climbed inside the small compartment and Scott secured the trap door. Before the elevator began its descent to the cargo area, Scott texted Skip.

We're rolling.

Skip left the truck running at the bow. A ramp from the large cargo opening bridged the gap between the ship and the dock. Skip helped Scott maneuver the table towards the truck.

"That must be some kind of special table to have to have a refrigerated truck for it. Just hold it right there," said the guard.

"Yeah, it's custom made with exotic woods, a gift of appreciation. We probably went over the top with the climate control for it, but we would hate to have it warp in this humidity," replied Scott.

The guard, along with his acute-sensed companion, slowly circumnavigated the table with the dog's nose millimeters from the base of the table. The Shephard exhibited a perplexed look on his face, but there were no barks or behavioral changes.

"Okay, you guys are good," said the guard.

With the truck running, Skip lowered the oversized power lift, and they slid the table onto the platform. The mechanism protested with a long squeak as it inched upwards. Inside, the pair guided the table up against the front wall and stretched a rope behind the legs. After locking the casters, Skip helped Scott down, secured the overhead door, and stepped inside the cab. With the back closed up, Skip moderated the freezing air streaming into the rear of the rolling refrigerator. Scott climbed in with a huge sigh, and they were moving.

Skip pulled next to his SUV in the parking lot and dropped Scott off. Scott followed the truck to a predetermined corner of the lot where Skip backed the truck up near the wall of a building. Leon slid open the latch and exited the compartment for the last time. Scott raised the overhead door, and the Zengmaster slid into the back of Skip's vehicle, quickly throwing on a dark t-shirt. Slouched down, Leon spoke with watery eyes.

"I can't believe I am in America. I am so grateful to you."

"We all pulled it off," said Scott. "Our future was in the hands of, or should I say the nose of that dog. His scent must have been overwhelmed with the pine."

Scott followed Skip over to the truck rental and arranged to have the table shipped to Hawthorne.

"Just keep it at the speed limit," suggested Scott. "Or at least make sure there are cars going much faster than we are,"

The drive up the Eastern seaboard was leisurely and uneventful for the New York bound trio. Scott and Skip split up the driving and they stopped for an overnight in North Carolina. Scott's paranoia took them off the beaten path, and far down the ladder in terms of lodging amenities. Skip's Escalade was conspicuous at the Ma and Pa motel where they settled. Here, no one would be asking Leon for any identification.

"You guys aren't some kind of agents are you?" asked the man at the front desk.

"Well you know we couldn't tell you that," said Scott.

Spring break in Scott's college days was the last time he had hunkered down in a place like this. The three sandwiched themselves into the room and there was a rap on the door. Behind a rickety rollaway was a stocky man who pushed a wobbly cot inside. Scott slipped him a fifty, receiving a dentally-challenged smile in return. As Skip carefully crawled onto bed, the apparatus cried for a shot of WD-40. When the first beam of morning light breached the limpid curtains, Scott roused his partners and they hit the road for the last leg of the journey.

Finally, after thousands of nautical miles, and thirteen hundred highway miles, a tinge of liquid glazed over Scott's eyes as they pulled into the driveway of his first home. For now, the suitcases were left in the SUV, and the front door opened before the trio reached the porch.

"This is Li, Li Zee," said Scott,

"Welcome. Our home is your home," replied Kate graciously.

Mark stepped up for his handshake with Leon. Nothing registered to him that it was the ex-champ. Leon's hair was short, unlike the mop top that used to flop around over his headband as he dominated play. Mark had watched videos of his matches, but that was far from his mind. Koji deliberately kept Leon a secret. He wanted to keep Mark focused, and if he had to send him home, it was better that Mark never knew he was coming.

"Do you play table tennis Li? Mark asked with smirks populating the faces of everyone behind him.

"Oh, I used to play more," replied Leon.

Leon reached into the right pocket of his shorts, and handed Mark a small soft wrapped package. The paper pulled off easily revealing a white headband with a *red Z* and a trailing *lightning bolt*.

"You're Leon Zeng! Said Mark with disbelief. "Wow. Thank you."

"It's Li Zee in this part of the world, and he is to remain a secret," said Scott with a firm tone.

Mark immediately picked up on the seriousness of that request, but it didn't shake him out of his star struck state.

"He's here to provide a little instruction, and no one is to know that he is here until we give the word," said Koji.

In 1971, American Glenn Cowan received a silk screen portrait from Chinese player Zhuang Zedong when he climbed aboard the Chinese team bus in Japan. This event was thought to be the catalyst for Ping Pong Diplomacy. This exchange, certainly would chill relations if the Chinese were to ever get wind of it.

It took months of planning, and stress to haul in the biggest and most elusive fish of them all. Now here he was, in the midst of a handful of people who were the only ones privy to his whereabouts. After some sandwiches, everyone headed down to the basement where Koji had spent time preparing both sides for play.

Although older, the spare table was in pristine condition. It was German made, green, and robust; tank-like in its construction. Koji loved it, and confirmed that the bounce coefficient of the surface mirrored the newer table in Mark's cove. It was a favorite possession of Koji, and he was quite enthused that the greatest player ever would be imparting his wizardry upon it.

"Over here first Leon," said Koji. "This is your new office."

Leon gave Koji a perplexed look.

Along with Leon, it was the first time Scott and Skip had seen the custom playing area designed to open up Mark's play and make him feel at home.

"It's Mark's home away from home," said Koji. Or should I say it's the Chinook-like nook. We had to ironically close up the space, to open up his game."

"Your creativity never ceases to amaze me Koji. Oh, and I think I know who did the murals. Very nice Leah. I'm thinking, I can reopen up club tonight around ten after everyone leaves. We will have it all to ourselves, hang out, and order some pizzas."

For now, the mood was chipper in the Yamaguchi house, but the kid from Albania, the other part of the package deal, was scheduled to arrive tomorrow. Scott figured an evening at the club would at least temporarily take everyone's mind off of him. He had still refrained from giving Jeton the scoop on Mark. Getting the news from Lukas would certainly infuriate Jeton more. The heat would come, but thousands of miles away. What could Jeton do about it? If he told the authorities about Leon, Lukas would not get trained.

Europe was getting stocked with a nice crop of talented junior players. Scott witnessed a couple first hand on The Ping. One from Poland, and one from Germany. Lukas seemed to plateau during the early teen years, the period when some players make a quantum leap. His father though, retained an overinflated estimation of his abilities, and this fed Lukas' ego. Jeton believed Leon could propel his son upwards into elite company. Scott, the keen evaluator of talent, was skeptical. He concluded that Lukas lacked some concrete skills, along with intangibles like work ethic, attitude, adaptability, and the ability to bounce back from adversity. Lukas was gifted, but it took more than that to become a world class player. Mark would tear into him tomorrow, a moment Scott and Koji were dreading.

The seven night owls piled into Skips vehicle and after the short ride waited for Scott to deactivate his club's security system. When he flipped an array of switches, the optimized assemblage of ceiling lights illuminated a sea of blue table tops, twenty feet below. The beautiful wood gymnasium floor gave slightly as the group walked in. Mark was completely awestruck. He had taken the virtual tours, and watched countless matches on *You Tube*, but this blew away all his expectations. The first club he was setting foot in, was the most prestigious in the United States, and it was a private gathering. Scott's voice echoed throughout the facility rousing Mark out of his thoughts.

"Take your time and look around."

Mark headed over to the multiple display cabinets which housed collectibles and antiques from the very early days of table tennis. Leah had been there innumerable times in her youth, but nestled in next to Mark, basking in his emotions. Leon joined the pair and Leah commented.

"Those paddles are made from sheepskin. The name *Ping Pong* was trademarked, so that game *Bing Bang* was a knockoff. Notice how formally everyone was dressed when they played."

"There's Scott's trophies when he was in high school," said Mark.

"That big room back there with additional tables can be reserved for private parties," said Leah. There's a big flat screen in there too. Why don't you guys go hit some?"

Mark and Leon walked back on into the main playing area. *Is this real?* Thought Mark. *I'm going to return the first ball that the best player in the world has hit on American soil…in one of the most famous clubs in the world.*

Two tables away, Skip and Koji rallied, while Leah dusted off her rusty game and hit balls with Scott. Mark and Leon gradually stepped up the pace of their shots with Leon gauging the limits of Mark's capability. There was just that little extra jump, generated from Leon's effortless flick, keeping Mark in a defensive mode. Skip returned from a short break in the office and walked over to Scott, who was now taking a breather himself.

"I saw a couple e-mails from people inquiring about a cruise next year."

I know I made it clear on The Ping that there wouldn't be one. But of course there were others who wanted to get on and couldn't. We'll have to put something on the website at the end of the cruise recap."

"No cruise will ever live up to that one," added Skip.

Mark and Leah exchanged shots for the first time. She hardly picked up her paddle anymore, but had a zip to her strokes when she wasn't goofing around. At a party, these two would be show stoppers—like the couple that can really dance, one by one sending the fakers out to the perimeter. The ball danced between these two in rhythmic fashion, and Mark never stepped on Leah's toes. How awesome, Mark thought, finding a girl who could play. After the break for pizza, the action wound down with some friendly doubles. Scott closed things down at 1:00 a.m.

CHAPTER 13

◆————————————————————◆

THE EXCHANGE STUDENT

L eah peered outward from the west facing window of the upstairs studio.

"That's him," she said. "He looks to be a little shorter than you, and less buff of course."

Mark moved next to her for the birds-eye view, brushing his cheek against hers. At the base of the long driveway, Lukas pulled one piece of luggage behind him, piggybacked with a sports bag.

"He's walking like he's got some attitude," said Mark.

"Oh yeah, he's confident all right. He insisted on making the trip here without any help."

"Scott never told me about him. Your dad waited until yesterday to tell me. When did you know about him and Leon?"

"I knew before the summer started, but dad told me to be quiet. Scott and my parents have visitors stay here sometimes, but not for very long. It's going to be weird up here with three guys, all from different countries. I can't wait to get up to Cornell, no offense," said Leah with a short laugh. "We better get downstairs for the *big* reception."

Leah was spot on about Lukas' stature, as the black-haired teen approached the front door. After a relaxing night at the club, the group waited in the living room and braced, ready to counterbalance the strong approaching personality. Three quick bursts from the doorbell caused Leah to flinch, and Koji opened the front door.

"Welcome," said Koji. "This is my wife Kate. We will be making sure things go well for you. That's my daughter Leah, and you are familiar with Scott and Skip." Koji continued.

"This is Mark. He is going to be training with us and going to school at Hawthorne as well."

"What's your rating?" asked Lukas.

"I don't have one," answered Mark.

"Then you must be a basement player," said Lukas as the pair shook hands.

"Actually I'm a garage player," said Mark, well aware of the derogatory term used to label inferior players.

"At least that's higher than a basement." quipped Lukas. "Are you Leah's boyfriend or something?"

At that point, Mark just bit his tongue, itching for the opportunity for his paddle to do the talking. Lukas progressed through the rest of the introductions with his eyes consistently trying to get a lock on Leah's pupils. Leah elusively scattered her glances around the room, with Mark picking up on this dynamic.

"You know who this is," said Koji extending his hand towards Leon.

"Yes, of course. The best player in the world, well years ago."

"He is going by Li," said Koji. "I was told that your dad filled you in that he is to remain a secret."

"I got that."

"I have to take care of some business at the club. I'll be back around in the next few days to see how things are going," said Scott.

"Nice seeing you again Lukas."

"Lukas, let us show you around," said Kate.

The upstairs orientation was short. Lukas threw his things down on the bed and texted his dad saying he arrived okay at the Yamaguchi's. He wanted to get right down to action in the basement. Koji led the small procession of three players into the deep finished substructure. Lukas stepped into Mark's custom practice area.

"You guys do graffiti down here?"

"They're murals," replied Mark.

"We could do some hip hop stuff. Tirana has it all over. The outside wall of our old club was covered in it.

"I'll warm you up on this side Lukas," said Koji.

Mark and Leon stepped up to the partially enveloped table and began to rally. Embedding into the soft sponge rubber, and recoiling off the multi-ply paddles, their balls echoed with the distinctive *tock* of well struck projectiles. Lukas made occasional glances to the other side of the room, and tuned his ears in that direction, as he exchanged shots with Koji.

Leah pulled up a stool to watch her dad and Lukas. The best young player in Albania was cocky, and ready for action.

"Let me dust off the garage kid," said Lukas.

The dreaded moment had arrived. Mark walked over to the other side of the basement.

"Let me see your paddle," requested Lukas.

Mark laid it on the table as Lukas inspected both sides.

"Mark V. Did your grandfather hand this down to you?"

"It's brand new."

"Well, in case you wanted to know, I'm using *Tenergy*.

"Of course," replied Mark.

Mark was well versed in the properties of this rubber that some classified as the world standard. It's near the top of the price range, and is known for its catapult effect, explosiveness, and the large amount of spin that can be generated from it. Koji and Leon pulled up stools alongside Leah.

As the pair ramped up the customary forehand and backhand exchanges, Lukas' face reflected his concern that this was no kid right out of the basement, or the garage for that matter. The warmups ended, and Mark pointed at Lukas' empty right hand beneath the table, giving the first serve to Lukas. The best of five games was now underway.

From the first ball put into play, Mark was flawless with precise authoritative strokes. With Mark taking the first two games 11-5 and 11-4, the shoulders of Lukas slumped. He was told he had the potential to be the best player in Europe if he applied himself. Out of nowhere, he was blindsided by an unranked player.

Not possessing the swagger and demonstrative nature of some young players enabled Mark to remain poised and even keeled. Lukas was the mercurial type, his emotions rode the highs and lows of each point. In game three, Mark undetectably eased off his play, and finished the match with an 11-7 victory. Not wanting to express any favoritism, the three onlookers clapped in a subdued manner, as if to give credit to both players. The boys exchanged a quick token handshake, and Lukas started up the stairs. The nightmare scenario was underway.

"I'm going to head upstairs and lay down for a while," said Lukas.

"No problem. You've had a long day," said Koji.

Up in his room, Lukas picked up his cell.

"Dad".

"Hi. What's up?"

"So there's this kid staying here that's sixteen, and he is also going to train with Koji and Leon".

"Mr. Kobara didn't tell me anything about him, replied Jeton".

"Yeah well he beat me 11-4, 11-5, and 11-7,"

"That's crazy. What's his name?"

"Mark Linderman."

"Let me look him up here, hold on—I don't see him anywhere in the USATT or ITTF rankings".

"He said he had no rating, said Lukas."

"I'll call Mr. Kobara and see what this is all about."

"Okay Dad."

Jeton got right back on the phone to Scott. Scott answered casually.

"Hey Jeton, what's going on? I saw Lucas, and he looked unscathed from his long journey."

"Yeah, well cut the crap. Who's that kid?"

"Oh, you mean Mark. He just kind of fell out of the sky into my lap."

"You had to know about him before we got Leon out of the country. No kid is going to appear out of thin air and handily beat a junior champion. I can tell by Lukas' voice, he is bummed."

"A large dose of healthy competition between the two can raise both their levels of play," added Scott.

"Very funny. I think you should pay for deceiving me, the emotional distress you have inflicted. Well, let's see. Should I contact the Chinese Embassy, or Immigration and Customs Enforcement? Or, you have helped out my club before, and the mechanism is already in place to transfer funds. How about ten thousand a month to make sure that Leon remains undiscovered, and that you are able to play table tennis outside of a prison recreation facility. If Lukas is able to make it to the top, I might be willing to absolve you from your monthly obligation."

"Don't forget your involvement in this as well Jeton."

"It would be tough to trace me to it, and I think the Chinese would thank me as a matter of fact."

"You would take down the Yamaguchi's as well."

"Take Leon over to your house if you are concerned about them."

"I can move him around and you would look pretty foolish if they couldn't find him."

"I have eyes and ears there now."

CLICK.

Scott immediately texted Skip.

Hey Skip, meet me over at the club right after it closes. Bring your wheel barrel, a tarp, and all your power saws.

When Skip arrived, he wheeled his tools into the storage area.

"What's up?" Asked Skip.

"Things changed fast."

"Explain."

"When Jeton found out about Mark kicking Lukas' butt, he broke bad. He was livid that I didn't tell him about Mark. Now he is blackmailing me. He is threatening to call the Chinese Embassy or ICE to expose Leon if I don't send him ten thousand a month."

"So what are you going to do?"

"First, I want you to help me turn this custom table into some expensive firewood. Fortunately, I just kept it here in storage and didn't show it off."

"Some guys are going to be asking about it."

"I'll tell them there was some kind of hidden bug infestation and we had to destroy it. Anyway, I was talking to an attorney friend about options for Leon. He said that asylum is not easy to get, but the Chinese have the highest success rate of all nationalities in this country. Leon could always illegally integrate into society, but that is more difficult here than it is in the city. There he might be able to just coalesce into a neighborhood, but I'm sure that's not what he wants. I think he wants to do it right, and he has one year to petition for asylum. Once he comes forth and applies, he does risk denial, and exportation during his application proceedings."

"He will have to decide that. So, are you going to pay Jeton?"

"Well, initially yes. I am going to find the best lawyer I can for Leon. Win or lose, the payments would stop, but of course I want Leon to become a citizen."

Standing at opposite ends of the masterpiece, the two friends secured their dust masks and slipped on their safety glasses,

"Maybe we should wear these," suggested Scott, handing Skip a pair of lime green ear plugs. "Let's keep the cuts about six inches wide."

Both men plugged their extension cords into separate outlets, and picked up their circular saws.

"Gentlemen, start your engines," joked Scott.

With that, the whir of two saws swirled around the concrete walls. Clouds of sawdust filled the air, as the aromatic evergreen released its amazing scent. After an hour, the hacked up table was unrecognizable. Skip rolled a couple wheelbarrow loads out to his SUV and both men scooped piles of sawdust into snow shovels and dumped them into a lined can. Scott fired up the *Shop Vac*, and finally at midnight, the room was clean, but the smell would linger for days.

"Drop that load in my backyard tomorrow," said Scott. "Just possessing that rare wood makes me nervous. Let's set up a burning ceremony at the fire pit tomorrow night. I'm sure Leon will want to come, and we can discuss options with him."

"There's some small blocks over there," said Skip.

"Maybe I'll do something with them sometime. They're going in the safe for now."

Upstairs in the Yamaguchi's studio, an uncompleted game of *Risk* sat on the table. Leah carefully moved the board to the counter and spread out her final preparations for Cornell. The guys were back at it in the basement. Koji snapped Lukas out of his initial funk, and kept the boys away from keeping score when they did spar. Most of the time, Leon and Koji alternated with the pair. In the midst of practice, a voice echoed down the basement stairs and pierced through the rapid-fire.

"Koji." said Scott. "Take a break."

Koji followed Scott up the stairs and out into the front yard.

"Has Jeton been in touch with you?"

"No he hasn't."

Scott revealed Jeton's about-face.

"Do you think he would expose us," asked Koji.

"I have to respect him, and pay until we get things locked up. Tomorrow evening, you, Leon, and Skip can come over. We'll burn the firewood, and discuss things. I'll get a recommendation for an immigration attorney."

The next day, dusk faded into darkness. The four adults settled into Scott's tree-lined yard, pulling their chairs up to the oversized fire pit. A half-dozen wadded up paper balls sat beneath a layer of twigs compacted by a pile of the exotic crisscrossed boards.

"Okay Leon, you have the honors. One, two, three." said Scott.

Leon struck the elongated match and walked around the pit igniting three of the paper wads. Quickly the flames shot skyward into the kindling beneath the pine. Scott stood up with a shot glass in his hand. Raising it up, he signaled to the other three to follow suit.

"Here's to a new beginning, a new life for Leon…and the sweet smell of victory soon to be upon us."

The four threw back their shots as the brightness intensified. The fast burning pine snapped and crackled, releasing a distinct fragrance like nothing like they had experienced.

"Only a rich person could afford to use this stuff as firewood," joked Skip.

"What an awesome smell," said Koji.

"The guys at the club were looking a little perplexed today as the odor from all the sawdust crept out into the playing area," said Skip. "I think they bought your *bug* idea."

"Good," said Scott. "So Leon, I know Koji talked to you about working towards citizenship. I discussed this with immigration attorney today, and he said that one third of the people who are granted asylum, come from China. I told him you were denied a passport for no apparent reason, and you were experiencing mental anguish for leaving the national table tennis program. Also, I told him how much you were working on your English. So he is willing to represent you. Once you start the process, you are letting our government know you are here. So if you don't win your case, you can be sent back."

"I see. I trust you. I want to do what is right."

"Okay. I think everyone wants it that way," said Scott.

The evening rolled along with Leon and Koji exchanging stories of their competitive youthful days. Skip and Koji had heard about all of Scott's travels to foreign clubs, so he only retold a couple for Leon. As it got closer to midnight, Scott piled one last load of the Tasmanian conifer onto the pile for a spirited grand finale.

"That's it. When this burns down, it's time to call it a night."

The embers dimmed, the visitors exited, and the table was history.

CHAPTER 14

THE PING PONG CLUB

The day before Leah would be moving into her dorm, her and Mark slipped out on the bikes late morning.

"Let's ride into Pleasantville," Leah suggested. "It's about three miles. There's a sandwich shop and a small book store there. I want to get something to read for the trip up to school. Then we can ride over to Whippoorwill Park and eat."

"My dad gets all his books here," said Leah as they entered. He wants to help keep them in business."

"What are you getting?"

"*The Distance Between Us*. It's supposed to be a fast and light read."

After stepping into the sandwich shop. Leah snugged her book and the food into her bike pack, and the pair rolled four miles east to the park.

"It's awesome here," said Leah. "Scott lives nearby. Further in, there's a stream that flows through. Let's go find a spot."

Alongside the stream, the two sat down and Leah broke the silence.

"You'll like Hawthorne. It's a little diverse since it's a public school. Some people jump into cliques right away because they want to be accepted, but I never did. There's a ping pong club, and I joined for a year. I wanted to do different things. I did art, cheerleading, robotics. I took karate and volunteered. It's a good place to meet people, and nobody looks down on what you do. If you join the ping pong club, Dad said he doesn't want you showing off all your stuff. A few kids in the club play at Scott's since their dads do, so they are pretty good. Sometimes there's a small crowd watching at lunchtime in the winter.

"Who is your roommate going to be at Cornell?"

A girl from the Chicago suburbs."

"You're not on your phone much."

"I like my space, and I like nature. My friends know that. It's more fun sometimes to tell them things in person, like this, maybe, if it's okay."

Leah leaned over and looked at Mark eye to eye, stopping six inches from his face. Mark proceeded with caution. His internal traffic light flashed green, and externally, red permeated his cheeks. The teens breached the intersection with a slow soft collision. No damage, nobody's fault, no need to report it. Leah eased back from the bond, and reached for the sandwiches.

"I wish we could stay here until dusk," said Leah, as they finished eating. That's when you might hear the call of the Whippoorwill. You have to check out the Ornithology Lab at Cornell sometime."

"Definitely."

"We better get back because my parents will be pissed if we start packing late. Skip is dropping off his big SUV in an hour for us to use."

The wooded two lane roads became busier in mid-afternoon. Mark just floated along, unfazed by the cars disrespecting his personal space. The pair finally got to more bike-friendly streets and finally arrived at the base of the long driveway.

"Bad news is out shooting hoops," said Leah. "He must have stopped dribbling because I didn't hear anything."

The embers had long ceased radiating from their faces, but Lucas gave them a suspicious look and spoke sarcastically.

"Thanks for inviting me. Where did you guys go?"

"Bird watching," Leah answered quickly.

"Sounds boring."

Skip's vehicle sat under the carport with the rear hatch raised. Leah's weepy-eyed parents played a slow motion game of horizontal *Tetris*, sliding in the first set of boxes that the boys carried down. Leah's minimalist nature made the load up easy. Lastly, Koji secured Leah's bike on the carrier, and rubbed his hands together.

"Except for some incidentals tomorrow morning, that's it. You guys can sleep in a little bit, and then Leon will work with you. We'll be back in the afternoon tomorrow. We have two weeks of really intensive training to get in before school starts. Then we'll work out a new schedule. I think tonight is a carry-out one," said Koji.

Mark rose early to see Leah walk out and step into the SUV. He watched the vehicle slowly exit down the long driveway. Leah would only be a couple hundred miles away, but that could zoom to a couple thousand if he didn't stick to his regimen. So he stayed motivated, gradually lessening his vengeance towards his original detractors. Koji was right. It was someone who cared, that was now driving him.

Like he had done for the last two weeks, Mark rose before the others, grabbed an energy bar, and hit against the robot. He removed the one hanging sheet depicting the handful of Montana students, no longer drawing energy from the negativity. Koji was still trying to keep Lukas motivated, constantly telling him, you are the best young player in your country, and you can expand that.

The last full weekday of practice was upon them, school would start tomorrow.

The next morning, three blocks from the house, four teens climbed aboard the yellow bus before Mark and Lukas stepped up. A couple girls waved to each other enthusiastically, but most were fixated on their screens, or peering out as music leaked from their buds. After the short ride, the expansive glass and steel school entrance reflected the morning sun as the first buses rolled in. Thanks to Leah, Mark's first day jitters were tempered, but he wasn't used to walking into such an impressive modernistic structure. His intimidation waned as he joined the mix of students in the hallways. At the lunch break, Lukas was already mixing it up with a couple of girls. He had his European panache in full gear, and the two juniors were eating it up. When school ended, Mark was walking towards the buses when he heard Lukas' voice.

"Hey Mark, c'mon, hop in."

Mark squeezed into the back seat of the subcompact, side by side with a long-haired brunette. Before she even said her name, she fully extended her arm between the two front seats, and moved her head next to his. Instantly, the two faces were captured on her phone, side by side, filling her entire screen.

"I'm Sophie. That's my friend Carly."

"I'm Mark."

"Lukas says you're from Montana, and awesome at ping pong."

"Yeah, but he's the junior champion of his country."

The sub compact whipped away, with Mark scrunched tightly against the door. In less than ten minutes the vehicle sped up the Yamaguchi's driveway.

"Let's go inside," said Lukas to the two girls.

"Not a good idea," said Mark.

"Are you the gatekeeper of the house now?" asked Lukas sarcastically.

"Bye," the girls said in succession, picking up on the tone that had quickly turned negative. Sophie jumped in the front seat, and they roared off.

"What's the matter with you?" asked Lukas. "They would have just hung out in the basement and watched us practice."

Mark didn't answer, and after a peanut butter sandwich went downstairs. Leon and Koji were setting up some drills and practicing.

"No homework tonight," said Mark.

Lukas sauntered into the basement with some bad body language and an unwillingness to warm up with Mark in a moderate fashion. His returns were impractical and consistently hit the ball as hard as he could.

"Did you have a bad day today?" asked Koji.

"School was fine," replied Lukas.

Koji stepped over to hit with Lukas to help tame the irritated teen. With a dispirited tone overhanging the practice, Koji terminated the session early.

"Come back down after dinner," said Koji. "Teens," he murmured.

Upstairs, Mark was in the studio surfing with his tablet when Lukas walked in carrying his laptop.

"See, look at this. Even though you were so rude in the car, Sophie still posted the selfie of you two on her Facebook page."

Mark went back into his room and in a rare move, punched his pillow. As pissed as he was, he refrained from hitting any hard surface. The defroster wires behind him and Sophie made it obvious they were in the back seat together. Mark's naturally warm smile transcended his uncomfortableness with the situation. He had hardly said a word to Sophie, yet he looked like her boyfriend. The next day, Lukas mingled with the two girls during lunchtime, when an Asian senior walked over to him.

"Dude. Are you Lukas?"

"Yeah."

"I'm Yuan. Follow me to 110 across from the gym. The ping pong club is going on. We heard you were coming to our school. Here, use my paddle. The club plays on Tuesdays at lunchtime, and Thursdays after school for two hours. The rest of the days at lunch, the tables are open to all the students."

Lukas tepidly obliged, and walked over with the two girls following along. Yuan was the president of the club with twenty members, and sported a solid 1700 ranking. About forty kids surrounded the table, including Mark. Yuan grabbed his backup paddle and put a ball in play to Lukas. Lukas gradually ramped up his strokes to where he had Yuan on the defensive, drawing applause from the club members, other students, and a couple faculty members. Lukas' attitude was on the blasé side, and after ten minutes headed out with the girls. Mark, for now just observed the action, and overheard a couple girls commenting on Lukas.

"That European is taking out the trash, and the recycling together."

Hearing that, Mark immediately flashed back to his selfie with Sophie, now desperately wanting it off of her Facebook page. He rode the bus home, and with a light homework load, decided to go downstairs for an hour of practice. Lukas straggled in, an hour after Mark, and went right upstairs.

"What's up with Lukas?" asked Koji.

"Girls, I guess," said Mark. I'm going to check out the Ping Pong Club."

"The competition is going to be very easy, but like Leah said, it's a good social activity. Remember, Scott wants to keep you out of the spotlight for now. So take it easy on them, and don't reveal a lot of details. Everyone will eventually know you are living here, so they will think that is the reason you play so well."

After school on Thursday, Lukas booked right out with the girls, and Mark walked into the Ping Pong Club. As he walked in he was greeted by Yuan.

"I'm Yuan."

"Mark."

"Good, you've got your own paddle. Oh, Mark V rubber."

"Yeah, I picked it because of the name."

"I doubt it. That combo is about a hundred bucks, and you can't get it at any sporting goods store. I bet you're sneaky good. Why don't you hit some balls with Melanie at the corner table?"

Melanie was a cute blonde girl with medium length hair. She was there for the social aspects, the guys. Her play was rudimentary like a lot of the players there, and definitely by Mark's standards. Mark could carry on a conversation, look around, and still effortlessly return the ball precisely to the same spot, over and over. He was unlike anyone Melanie had ever played with. She was mesmerized by this connection, and their eyes alternated between the bouncing ball and each other's. Yuan observed them for a while and stepped over.

"Why don't you hit with Stephanie."

Stephanie was an Asian girl who had just got her ranking above 1000. Mark stepped up his play commensurately with her level, alternating top-spin forehands and backhands with a goal to give her just what she could handle. Finally, Yuan sent Mark over to play Dylan, the second best player in the club next to Yuan. When they finished, Yuan and Dylan gathered with Mark.

"Where do you play?"

"Garages and basements, mostly."

"No way. Do you know Lukas, the exchange student player?"

"Yeah. I don't know if he will want to belong to the club, being so good," said Mark evasively.

"Come back Tuesday at Lunchtime," said Yuan.

"No doubt."

Mark was feeling pretty good about himself and texted Leah when he got home.

Hey. How's school?

Really intense, right from the start. I joined ultimate Frisbee, and maybe I'll get into an engineering club. The table tennis club here is awesome, but I'm going to hold off for now. They usually do well in tournaments against other schools.

Nice. I joined the club at Hawthorne.

Cool.

What about Lukas?

He stepped in during lunchtime and just played ten minutes. The players knew who he was. They don't know anything about me though. He hasn't been practicing a lot.

How come?

Girls.

Already? I'm coming home next weekend, so maybe we can hang out, if you haven't found somebody yet. LOL.

I think Lucas tried for me. LOL. Not my style.

Anyone I know?

Two girls named Carly and Sophie.

No way. Trouble squared. I bet they jumped on him right away when they found out he wasn't from around here.

Thanks for telling me. See you next week.

Bye.

Scott's surprise unveiling of Mark smashed Jeton, but Lukas was moving on fast from his beating. He quickly immersed himself in the distractions of American life, and his father was helping fuel it. Chunks of Scott's first payment to Jeton were being recycled right back into the pockets of Lukas. And he flaunted it, figuratively waving the dollars right in Scott's face. Carly's beater always sported a full tank, and the trio could be seen hanging out at Starbucks after school. Next week it was Manhattan, with the train fare, dinner, and concert tickets all courtesy of Scott. Meanwhile, Jeton had no idea of his son's growing apathy towards table tennis.

Early Saturday afternoon, a horn honked outside the Yamaguchi residence. As Mark was heading back downstairs, Lucas passed him on his way out the door.

"How can you play table tennis when there's so much to do?"

Mark just looked at him and headed into the basement thinking, *that's easy to say when somehow you've got money, and you have already been the junior champ of a country.*

Over the weekend, Lukas did not enter the basement once. Koji assumed he was done with table tennis for the academic year there. Saturday, Koji and Mark went over to Scott's club to watch some top talent play in his monthly tournament. Yuan, Dylan, Stephanie, and a few other members of the school club were there to watch the action. Yuan walked over to Mark and Koji who were sitting together.

"Do you know Mr. Yamaguchi?" asked Yuan

Koji immediately answered.

"He's staying at our house for this school year, and maybe next year too."

"No wonder you're so good with Koji and Lukas there. Where's your parents?"

"In Montana," answered Mark, figuring it would appear dubious if Koji spoke for him.

"Dude, you must be serious about your game. How did you find out about him?"

Koji darted in again, tailoring the backstory.

"Actually Mr. Kobara, got in touch with me and he asked me if I might be interested in having another player at the house. Since Lukas was coming, I thought it would be good for him to always have a sparring partner around. It's nice to have people with such diverse backgrounds living with us."

Between matches, Scott walked over to the bleachers and sat down for a minute.

"How are things going?" Scott asked, which was code for how was the training coming along?

"Couldn't be better," said Koji.

"How about these matches today?"

"Great," said Mark.

"I've got to get back to my office before the next match starts," said Scott.

Mark paid attention how Koji carefully managed the facts. Koji looked so honest, and spoke so convincingly, that he could get away with being evasive. After the last match, Koji took Mark over to a yogurt place where they sat at a tall round table. Koji leaned over to Mark and spoke.

"You are going to get asked a lot of questions now that you are meeting more people at school. The only three things you have to avoid are, the cruise ship, Leon, and immediately demonstrating how well you can play. You'll have to dance around a question here and there. If anyone is coming over, let us know so we can keep Leon under cover. That's all I can think of. We want you to live as normal of a life as you can."

"No problem. Thank you for everything, you guys are so nice."

"It's our pleasure."

Over the years, Scott became one of the most prominent names in the table tennis community. It was impossible to overlook his contributions to the game, and overlook him to be on the planning committee for Ping Pong Diplomacy II. It was just in its embryonic stages, but Scott was in there scratching and clawing, establishing his presence. Right now, Scott continued to keep Mark under wraps and out of the club scent. Mark was making huge strides under the tutelage of Koji and Leon, and pounding the table for a competition while grooming a hot shot kid, might not sit too well with the committee. When details like location and dates gradually got cemented into place, the young star would emerge.

At lunchtime on Tuesday, Mark walked into the Ping Pong Club room. Yuan walked up to him.

"You know, everyone wants to play you."

"That's funny. Nobody wanted to play me in Montana. Nobody really played much at all."

There was a renewed buzz in the club, and four new players came on board. Scott donated a pair of tables when he purchased new ones. The graceful nature of Mark's game had an infectious nature to it. From a power standpoint, he hadn't even taken it out of first gear, and no one there had a clue what he could unleash.

A rainy Saturday morning Mark flipped through the images his parents sent him from their new house in Billings.

Mark hopped on Skype.

"How do you like our new place?" asked his mom.

"Cool. The garage looks huge."

"Two and a half cars," said his dad.

"Where's my table?"

"We are still living out of boxes here. Don't worry, your table and ball machines are in storage. We can set it up fast," said Candice."

"How are things going there?" asked his dad.

"The kids all accept me, and the Yamaguchi's have been so nice. I joined the ping pong club at school, and everyone wants to play me, not like—you know where."

"Girls?" asked his mom.

"Just the one."

"Well if the weather is not crazy during Christmas, or maybe during spring break, you can come out here. We're not far from the airport at all now," said his Dad.

"Okay. I'm going to head down and practice. Talk to you soon."

"Love you."

"You too."

Lukas had not appeared at the Ping Pong club since his short exhibition, and Yuan was intent on not having Mark just ghost away as well. Thursday, Mark walked into the club to help set up the tables and Yuan stepped up to him.

"You know, I'm into a couple other activities and need to focus on my college research. How would you like to be *president* of the club?"

"I don't really know what to do."

"Neither did I, but it kind of runs itself. I'll fill you in, and Dylan knows as much as I do."

"Sure," answered Mark humbly.

"Listen up everyone." Called out Yuan. Quiet overcame the room, and Yuan stood next to Mark. "We have a new president of the ping pong club—Mark Linderman!"

The two players shook hands, with a loud and enthusiastic round of applause, the transfer of responsibility was complete. Up front, a few members snapped some images before the action on the tables began. When the two hour session ended, a small crowd hovered over the snack table and Melanie squeezed her way up to the front, brushing against Mark. She grabbed two cupcakes, smiled, and handed one to Mark.

"Here, have this before they're all gone."

"Thanks," said Mark.

The physical confines of his garage were gone, but confines of a different sort were upon him. Bringing another girl in his life would completely change the tone at the Yamaguchi's. He pushed the entire cupcake into his mouth and eased next to Yuan and a small group.

Mark never cancelled his Facebook account, but hardly ever looked at his page. For the first time in months, he got on after the club meeting and found the whole ping pong club requesting to be friends. Pictures of him playing and becoming the new president emerged, and immediately he was drawn back in, but managed to minimize his exposure.

Friday afternoon, Leah grabbed a ride back from Cornell from a sophomore who lived a couple suburbs over. Mark's training progress was way ahead of schedule, according to Koji. He absorbed his school work quickly, and was very efficient with his study time. So Mark and Leah hit the movies, restaurants, and took some lengthy bike rides. Lukas was never around. The pair stopped at a small café, sitting across from each other at a tall round table.

"In two weeks, it's family weekend at Cornell. Why don't you come along?" asked Leah.

"I'm in. What about Lukas though?"

"I don't know. Scott and my dad are pissed at him. My dad only talks to him when he has to, and I am sure that he doesn't want him staying at the house. I could see those party girls talking him into having people over. You know how perfect my parents keep the place. If it was trashed, they would be devastated. Scott's probably looking for an excuse to send him home, but not that one."

"Leon would be home, but I guess you can't expect him to be like a parent. He couldn't stop anything anyway,"

"All he could do was call us at Cornell, and wreck the weekend. I hate to warn my parents, but I know those girls. The thought of having them in our house, yuck. But it would suck to have him tagging along with us."

"Yeah, really."

In the adjacent suburb of Pleasantville, Scott and Leon sat in a conference room across from an immigration attorney. The trio collaborated, and finished combing over Leon's application for asylum. Ironically, while at the table, Scott's phone vibrated with a text from Jeton.

Have you forgotten something? I mean another ten big ones should have shown up here. I am sure your lifestyle and dreams are worth it.

The check's in the mail…as soon as I can find some stamps.

Very funny, Jeton answered, not sure if Scott was serious.

"Okay Leon," said the attorney. Once they receive this, then they will notify you when to come in to get interviewed and fingerprinted. Your application will be reviewed, and if you haven't gotten a decision in about six months, you can apply for a work permit. If anyone asks you how you got into the country, you don't have to answer."

"So I can walk around and not worry?" asked Leon.

"Yes, but we think you should keep a low profile. It is also very important that you don't tell anyone you have applied. One reason is for the security of your family members in your home country. There have been cases in some countries where one's family was threatened, and this put pressure on the applicant to return. I don't think you have to worry about it, but it's best to be safe.

"Yes sir."

Everyone shook hands, and Scott texted Koji.

Leon's application has been submitted. A big weight is off of our backs now, at least legally.

Regardless of the outcome, Scott would likely have a year or so to utilize the training services of the best player in the world.

CHAPTER 15

THE RAVE IN THE MAN CAVE

Leah was the dream daughter. The self-starter kind who could be left on cruise control. The Yamaguchi's were in uncharted territory when it came to Lukas. Over the course of the last month, he was coming home late, leaving food and dishes out, and his clothes were strewn about—reeking. Fortunately, it would be over when the school year ended, but Koji and Kate were quickly growing weary of his ways. Informing his dad was useless. He was ticked at everyone for duping him about Mark.

With a hoody obscuring the perimeter of his face, Lukas walked in at 11:30 on the Wednesday night before the family weekend at Cornell. Koji sat on a stool at the kitchen counter.

"Come here for a minute. Sit down," said Koji.

Lukas straddled the stool, looking askance with minimal eye contact.

"This weekend is a family weekend at Cornell. Why don't you join us and sample what American college life is like."

"I'm good."

"What do you mean, you're good?"

"I mean I'm good with what I have plans to do this weekend."

"Well let me tell you something my friend, you need to cancel those plans. If the school gets a whiff of your extracurricular activities, your stay here in this country will be done."

"Alright, alright."

Lukas slid off the stool and headed up to his bedroom. Koji peered around in all directions and reached into the back corner of a kitchen base cabinet. He extracted a small dusty bottle, unlabeled, and two-thirds full. The spirits took on the hue of slightly tarnished pennies, and Koji filled a shot glass. He splashed the contents into the back of his throat. After tucking the potion back in its secluded spot, he flipped the lights, and marched into the bedroom.

A class cancellation enabled Leah to grab a ride home on Thursday and slip in a visit to the dentist.

"I got a perfect checkup." Leah told her mom, walking into the kitchen. "Is he really coming tomorrow?"

"Yes. Because he is an exchange student and a minor, we are responsible for his well-being. If he stayed at someone else's house and something happened, our judgement would be called into question."

"Bummer."

It was a relatively warm October Friday morning. Mark and Lukas were cleared to be absent from school. Mr. and Mrs. Yamaguchi waited outside in the *grandpa-mobile* as Leah called it. Leah closely followed Mark to the driver's side of the car with her hands on his shoulders. She laughingly assisted Mark into the back seat like police suspect, and squished in behind her dad. With three hours of social discomfort ahead, Mark at least provided a physical buffer between Leah and the unruly guest. Three minutes elapsed with no Lukas.

"I left a detailed note, and food in the fridge for Leon," said Mrs. Yamaguchi.

"If Lukas didn't eat it all in the middle of the night," added Leah.

"No, I looked, and I made enough for an army anyway."

Just before Koji was ready to go back inside, Lukas leisurely headed over to the passenger side and slid in next to Mark.

"Did you lock the door behind you?" asked Koji.

"Yeah."

Lukas' hoody helped to obscure Leah's glances in that direction, and that was just fine with her. His mere presence set the awkward tone within. As they merged onto the highway, a combination of smells were emanating from Lukas' hoody. He showered, but this garment had been through a few too many parties. Koji prided himself on the quiet interior of his luxury liner, and was always reluctant to open the windows. Open windows would solve two problems for Mark, Lukas' odor, and his disdain for air conditioning. But without discussion on the matter, at five minute intervals, Koji would lower all four windows a tad for thirty seconds, and then raise them, over and over for the entirety of the trip. For the majority of the ride, all that could be heard, was the percussive hiss escaping from Lukas' ear buds.

Lukas lagged the group like a fifth wheel as they hiked around the campus, visiting libraries, student centers, and the Ornithology Lab. After a dinner in downtown Ithaca, it was off to the gym for a women's volleyball game. While Lukas went to the washroom, Koji engaged Mark.

"Leah is staying in our room at the hotel. You and Lukas will be together next door, so keep an eye on him."

"Sure."

The long dark driveway leading to the Yamaguchi's house was empty, but the rear patio was another story. Twenty bikes covered the concrete slab. The ones without kickstands were leaning against furniture or laying on their sides. Inside, the lower space dedicated to table tennis was now raging. Red cups and beer cans lined the perimeters of both ping pong tables, with some inevitably finding the floor. Two large trays of homemade tuna casserole were completely decimated. One girl became entangled in a mural, tearing it down from the ceiling. Teens danced to a mega boom box pumping out the decibels. With the basement door closed, only the lowest notes and their resonances leaked into the first floor. The bedrooms upstairs were audibly isolated from the subterranean bash. In his bedroom, oblivious to it all, Leon Zeng was fast asleep.

Outside on the patio, a half dozen loud inebriated teens went outside to smoke. Leon groggily started down the stairs to check out the noise. As he went into the kitchen, the reverberations from below breached the soles of his slippers, massaging his feet. Three sets of orange parking lights stealthily moved up the driveway in succession. The unannounced squads stopped, and four doors quietly opened and closed. With flashlights beaming, two officers exited one vehicle, and skirted along the side of the house to the patio. Just as Leon was about to descend to the basement, the front porch security light tripped, and the doorbell rang. Leon peered through the seeded glass sidelight, to observe a pair of blue silhouettes. As Leon opened the door, two larger than life officers monopolized the entrance.

Leon's heart raced. A two-way radio squawked from a policeman's chest.

"There's six underage teens back here, apparently under the influence."

Leon, without hesitation opened the storm door and let the officers in. His spotty facial hair gave him the look of an adult. One officer proceeded downstairs while one stayed up with Leon. When the basement door opened, the music and raucousness roared up the stairwell. As each circle of teens successively caught the presence of the blue uniform, the rowdy conversations throttled back to a stop, one by one. The boom box awkwardly blasted out the last of its gut-thumping bass, and finally, the closest teen fumbled for the off switch. There was silence. The two officers returned from outside and led the six teens down into the basement. With the partiers now reduced to mannequins, the men in blue had full command of the now quiet room.

Back upstairs, Leon was questioned.

"Do you live here?"

"Yes sir"

"Do you have identification?"

"No sir."

"Where are the owners?"

"They are at Cornell for the weekend."

"Go ahead of me down into the basement."

The officers proceeded to gather personal information from the shocked teens.

"Who bought all this beer?" asked one of the officers.

Of course there was complete silence. Upstairs, the policeman noticed a note on the kitchen counter and asked Leon.

"Is this the number of the owners?"

"Yes," answered Leon.

At 11:30 p.m. the movie was nearly ending in the Yamaguchi's hotel room, when Koji's cell buzzed and illuminated.

"Yes, this is Mr. Yamaguchi. We live there, but we don't own it. Yes. Yes, I see. Yes he does. The owner is about ten minutes away. I will call him and send him over there."

"What's happening?" Asked Kate.

"There was a rave in the man cave. I have to call Scott."

"Scott, we're in our hotel room in Ithaca and I got a call from the Hawthorne police that there was a party at the house. Can you head over? Leon is going to be held for questioning for supplying alcoholic beverages to minors."

"You've got to be kidding me. Alright, I'm leaving right now."

"I knew it," said Leah with a seething raised voice.

Koji debated going next door to tear into Lukas, but he wanted to salvage the rest of the trip, and waited to get the details from Scott. A half hour elapsed and Scott called, giving the rundown to Koji.

"Here's what happened," said Koji turning to Kate and Leah. "There were twenty teens, all on bikes, and it took place in the basement. A neighbor called when they heard loud kids outside. Leon was on the main floor when the police arrived, and obviously the only one there appearing to be over twenty-one. Nobody knew who he was, and he didn't produce any ID. When asked where they got the beer, some girl pointed at Leon. There's only minor damage in the basement, but it's a mess. The police took the kid's names, and didn't issue charges. They made sure everyone got a ride home."

"I know those girls were involved," said Leah.

Koji continued.

"Okay, tomorrow, not a word about this to Lukas. His phone will likely be blowing up with texts, and our silence should speak louder than anything we could yell at him. Leah, text Mark and let him know what happened before he gets it from someone else. Tell him he is not to bring it up."

Saturday's mood was strained, but the group slugged through the day's activities. Leah needed to catch up on her studies so she broke off mid-afternoon. Lukas texted non-stop with Carly on the way home, and finally Koji pulled into the driveway at 8:00 p.m. Once the overnight bags were set down in the foyer, Koji directed his wife and the two boys down into the basement.

"I swear I did not tell anyone to use this house. I only told someone the reason I couldn't go to their party, that's all."

"Someone singled out Leon as the one who provided the beer, and he could get in a lot of trouble for that, maybe even deported," said Koji.

"I'll clean all this up. I'll pay any damages. I'll do whatever I need to."

Lukas grabbed a box of garbage bags and began attacking the carnage. When everyone else was upstairs, he texted Carly.

Who told the cops that Leon bought the beer?

Oh, you mean that Asian guy that was there. Nobody knew who he was and he looked old enough. I didn't tell them anything.

The cops said someone pointed at him. You've got to go to tell them that it wasn't him.

Screw that. I'm not going to go talk to the police.

Screw you. I'm done. With a tap of his finger, one load of baggage was jettisoned into cyberspace. Mark broke from the angry trio upstairs, and headed downstairs to help out.

"Really, I didn't tell anyone to come over here, said Lukas."

"Watch who you hang with, and talk to."

The boys worked diligently until midnight and returned the next morning with rags and a mop. Mark climbed up and secured the torn mural to the ceiling.

"I think it's better down here now than before the party," said Mark. Hey, I'm thinking about volunteering at the food pantry to get some community service in. You want to go over there with me?"

"Yeah, I can check it out."

Early afternoon Sunday, the boys rode their bikes over to the last small brick building in the quaint business district on Commerce Ave.

"What brings you gentlemen in today?" Asked an older woman in the front lobby.

"We saw that you needed volunteers."

"Yes, in the worst way. If you have some time to help out now, I am by myself."

For the next two hours Mark and Lucas packed and unpacked boxes, and arranged items on shelves. After arriving home Lucas hit balls downstairs with Mark for the first time in almost a month. The door to the basement opened, and the first person to enter was Leon sporting a big smile. Scott followed in right behind him.

"He's clean."

"What happened?" asked Koji.

"They held him for questioning at the station, but didn't charge him while they investigated. Fortunately, one of the officers found a receipt stuck to the bottom of one of the cases of beer. It showed a large purchase the evening of the party. The cashier over at William's didn't recall seeing Leon, and after reviewing the surveillance video, the evidence technician discovered a large white male making a purchase at the time on the receipt. So, here he is. What a relief."

Leon took the whole ordeal in stride and dove right back into what he did best, fire table tennis balls at Mark. Things were back to rocking in the basement with a hot five hour practice session, interrupted only by a foot-long sandwich break.

Halfway through his sandwich Lukas said, "I think I'll join the ping pong club."

"That's a good thing," said Koji. "Sure, you can smash the ball past everyone, pound your chest, and alienate everyone. Or many years from now, some of the kids will be bragging how the Albanian junior champion was really cool and taught me these shots. Most kids won't play in tournaments, but at family reunions, they will be king of the hill. You won't know it, but you can carry that around with you. So only join because you want to meet people, help people, and have fun. Laugh when you are surprised with a lucky shot.

"I never thought of that."

"Look dude." Mark interjected. "I was nobody at school before

I joined this club. All I did in there was play to the person's level on the opposite side of the table, encourage them, and take an interest in their game. People in there have other talents, and they aren't ready to jam that down my throat."

"You sound like Koji, just joking," said Lukas.

"That's not a bad thing," said Mark. "Anyway, Leon. Lukas and I went over to the food pantry over on Commerce Drive and volunteered. Evelyn is still looking for help. She's there in the afternoon."

"I will check that out."

With lunch over the guys finished their session and Mark texted Yuan and Dylan.

Just a heads up. Lukas is coming to the club Thursday afternoon. So spread it around so he gets a good reception. I will try to be a few minutes late.

So with the boys back at school, Leon rode one of the Yamaguchi's bikes over to the pantry.

"Hello. My name is Li, and I would like to help out."

"Absolutely. How did you find out about this?" asked Evelyn.

"Mark Linderman told me. I am working to become a United States citizen."

"Oh yes, those boys really helped me out. If you work like they did, we will be in good shape. Our busy time of year is coming up and we are getting a lot of donations."

So while Mark and Lukas were at school, Leon not only stocked, organized, and cleaned.

"This back room hasn't looked like this in a long time, Li. I cannot thank you enough. Stop back anytime."

"Thank you Ms—"

"You can call me Evelyn."

Thursday after school, Mark and Lukas grabbed their backpacks before heading over to the ping pong club. The two juniors followed the sound of the bouncing balls into the club room. Mark held up his arms and the percolating din tapered off to quiet.

"Okay everyone. Lukas is going to join us so take advantage of having the junior champion of Albania."

A warm round of applause erupted and Lukas moved around to different tables, mellowing out his attitude and play, and taking keys from Mark's laid back style. The afternoon was a therapeutic one, one that both Mark and Lukas needed. At home, Lukas showered, threw his clothes in the laundry, picked up his room, and studied. After a dinner devoid of any tension, Lukas was right downstairs for the evening training session.

"Leon, how was the pantry today?" asked Mark.

"Very good. Very good."

"Did Evelyn give you some of her beef stew?"

"It smelled so good, but—"

"What?"

"The attorney told me that I cannot take anything for doing work. Not even food. That looks like I am working for something, and I am not able to do that yet."

"That stinks."

"She says Thanksgiving is coming up, so she will need me a lot."

CHAPTER 16

THE MAKINGS OF DIPLOMACY

Scott spent the last week in meetings in Washington D.C. Monday evening he walked into the Yamaguchi's house with a big smile on his face.

"Koji, open your laptop," he said.

Scott, the four players, and Mrs. Yamaguchi gathered around the kitchen island.

"Go to *The Post*, page three."

50th Anniversary of Ping Pong Diplomacy to be Held Here.

"Yeah. We got it done. It's going to be in the nation's capital on April 10th of 2021. That's less than eighteen months away. There's going to be the usual ceremonies, some original participants, and memorabilia. But the watershed event, the biggie, is that they agreed to a real competition.

With the news, a round of applause ensued.

"Hold on," Scott continued. "It's not going to be full blown team competition though, but it will be happening. They agreed to pit their top player against the top player in the United States in a one on one contest. The format will be the best of eleven games, the first player to win six games wins the match. It is going to be held at the spectacular Fichandler Stage located inside the Mead Center for American Theater."

"Awesome," said Koji.

"Yeah, it's almost exclusively used for theatrical performances, but the intimacy of the theater in the round makes it a fantastic venue for a table tennis. It holds around seven hundred, so the seats will not be plentiful. They're going to install temporary custom flooring and additional lighting. It's likely to be shown live on a national network, but that has to be negotiated."

"So how was it chosen?"

"I was there for the renovations in 2010. It was the last theater I was a consultant to before I hung up my headphones. I am very sentimental about that place. Once I suggested it, I didn't have to pound the table to convince anyone. The committee members fell in love with it when they saw it. When they heard it—perfection."

"How did they hear it?" asked Leah.

"It's the lack of hearing it I should say. I happened to bring my paddle and a ball inside, and gave them a demonstration. I told all the members to go up into the seats and close their eyes. I bounced the ball up and down on the paddle. They all said that they seemed to be able to pinpoint the location of the ball without seeing it. There's very few parallel surfaces, and that combined with the strategic placement of damping materials, creates the perfect balance between direct and reflected sound. I could go on and on."

"A perfect combination of your two passions in life," said Kate.

"So now what?" asked Koji.

"Well now we can get these guys out and playing at the club and in sanctioned competitions. Lukas, people know who you are, but Mark, we will ease you into it, but the word will spread fast. The Chinese are locked into the venue now. It's time to blindside them."

"Interesting," said Koji. "You'll be here for Thanksgiving, right?"

"Wouldn't miss it for the world," replied Scott.

Mark immediately texted Leah with the news.

An extreme skill set, humbleness, and consideration for others, contributed to the rising tide of Mark's popularity at school. The newbie to any prior social scene was flourishing in these uncharted waters. Lukas, who dove head first into the misbehavior pool, was now comfortably riding in Mark's wake. Mark was his last get out of jail free card, His new found conformity and humbleness paid off, as a fellow club member, Hannah, entered his world.

That afternoon Lukas got a text from his dad who had not received any money from Scott since the first payment.

What's going on there?

What do you mean Dad?

I mean I haven't heard from you lately.

Well the only big news is that some kids had a party here at the house while I was at Leah's college for a family weekend. Leon got taken into custody for buying beer for minors.

What?

Oh, he was released when they proved it wasn't him.

So he is back at the house?

Yes. He's volunteering and training us.

What else are you doing?

Oh, I'm practicing, and I joined the ping pong club at school.

Girls?

One.

I might not be able to send you so much money.

That's okay. I'll get by. Talk to you later.

Okay. Bye son.

The day before Thanksgiving Leah arrived home for the next five days. Leon wrapped up a busy month of volunteering, and would again step up his daily training regimen with the boys while they were off from school. Mark continued his upward trajectory, excelled at school, and grew his social following. Lukas would never challenge Mark in any department, but riding in his wake was a smooth and beneficial place to be.

Koji and Leon teamed up to work the teens into a freakish frenzy of drills, stoking up appetites for tomorrow's feast. So far, the culinary experience at the Yamaguchi's was beyond belief for the three young men. It was hard to believe that anything could eclipse it, but Mrs. Yamaguchi tried, and apparently succeeded. Leon and Lukas' first Thanksgiving knocked them out from overindulgence, while Mark fell victim to the second helpings as well. The disciplined Leah returned to her preparations for her exams, as she did for the rest of the long weekend. With her studying, and Mark practicing, the pair hardly interacted before she headed back upstate Sunday afternoon.

In the bright corner of her dorm lounge, Leah stretched out a new and ironed white sheet. With inspiration from her online tour of the Fichandler Stage, she outlined her most ambitious mural, envisioning herself looking down the aisle from the back row of the theater.

A mid-December dusting of snow greeted the early risers. Leah was on break, not beginning her second semester until the middle of January. The tension that hung in the in the Yamaguchi's home for months, had eased with the young Albanian's behavioral makeover. Mark elected to hang around Hawthorne for the Christmas break. The three boys were up and sitting at the kitchen island while Kate and Koji worked in concert to prepare breakfast. They were never on break, but made things look easy, and loved every moment of it.

Clumps of pre-cut vegetables sat on a cutting board, accompanied by chorizo and a blend of cheeses. Both parents cracked eggs and each attended to a separate pan on the stove.

"He's the designated flipper," said Kate.

Koji grabbed the non-stick skillet and flipped the first humongous hodgepodge into the air. The saucer shaped staple completed its single revolution, and softly nestled into the pan.

"That was one of the small things on his bucket list," said Kate. "And I can tell you, the early attempts ended up in the bucket."

Kate tossed in some chorizo and cheese, folded the fluffy entrée over, and presented it.

"The first one to dive in has to walk out and get the mail," said Kate.

Leon jumped at the first offering and dove in.

"I like the snow," he said between bites.

"That's because you they don't get that much where you came from," said Koji.

Leon returned from the street with a small bundle of letters. His first footsteps were halfway filled with snow as the flurries intensified.

"Here's something for you Mark," Leon said, handing him an envelope.

Mark tore off the ends.

"My USATT member card."

"Your member number is a lot higher than mine," said Koji. "I must be old. Scott is kicking off the year with one of his big tournaments in January, and we need to get you guys in."

"Which events should we enter?" asked Mark.

"Scott and I were talking. Lukas, we think the U2400 is good for you. Some people will know who you are, and that looks to be right. We don't need you two to play against each other, so we were came up with the U2200 for you Mark. You are obviously much higher than that, but Scott wants you to fly under the radar for a while. If you entered the Open, you would attract way too much attention. Scott wants to turn up the temperature one degree at a time, so to speak. Mark, you won't be eligible for any prizes since it is your first tournament, but you will establish a rating, and get some valuable experience. Scott's going to pick up the fees and sign you guys up."

"Thank you," said both Mark and Lukas.

"Leon, you are going to have to wait a bit."

"Are you playing Koji?" asked Mark.

"No. I'm going to help with the administrative stuff. Keep the brackets updated, figure out who plays where, and do some umpiring. Oh, and of course watch you guys when I can. How about we head downstairs."

Koji pulled Mark off to the side privately while Leon and Lukas were hitting balls.

"Scott suggested that you take it easy in the tournament. Just do what you have to, to get the wins."

"I got it."

CHAPTER 17

THE HEADBAND

The Yamaguchi's celebrated Christmas in a traditional manner with a live tree and an average spattering of lights outdoors. Like Thanksgiving, seven would be seated for the feast, and after dinner, gifts were exchanged. Leah got Mark a sharp warm-up suit, while he presented her with a silver watch. Scott was his over the top self with everyone's cards bountifully stuffed with greenbacks, Mr. and Mrs. Yamaguchi would be spending a weekend of their choice in Manhattan.

Leah was up in the studio working diligently on her secret mural. Nine days loomed before she had to return to Cornell. Hawthorne High was back in session. Mark and Lucas walked into Tuesday's lunchtime ping pong club session. Yuan quickly stepped over to the pair.

"I see you guys are signed up for Scott's tournament this weekend. I'm playing. So is Dylan, Stephanie, and Abby. Most of the club is going to be there supporting us."

"I saw that," said Mark. "You're in the U1800 and U2000."

As Mark and Lukas walked out of the club, Lukas turned to Mark.

"You know that Melanie girl was asking me questions about you."

"Like what?"

"You know, if you are seeing anyone."

"What did you say?"

"I didn't say no, and I didn't want to just say yes, because you know, she is really hot. So I just said that you had mentioned someone from another school, but you didn't see her very often."

"That's cool."

Saturday morning, Mrs. Yamaguchi, Mark, Lukas, Leon, and Leah headed over to the Hawthorne Table Tennis Center for the monthly four star tournament. Mark was pumped for his first sanctioned event. Leon slumped down in the back seat, and exited the car after everyone else to avoid any association with the Yamaguchi's. The general population wouldn't have a clue who he was, but around a premier table tennis facility, astute players could make a connection. So Leon, donned a New York Knicks cap, tinted glasses, and patches of facial hair. Over the course of the morning, twenty-four teens from the ping pong club filtered in to watch the event.

Lukas had the first match, and drew a small crowd as the word spread who he was. The U2400 was only one level below the Open category, and juniors competing against older guys always generated interest. Lukas was rusty, but drew from the support from the ping pong club, his girlfriend, and survived his match against the 2175 ranked player, winning three games to one. This boded well for Mark.

It's uncommon in the table tennis world, when an unrated player enters, or really belongs in an event rated above the master, or 2000 level. Mark was one of these rare birds, self-directing a large part of his upward trajectory, and taking a circuitous route to this tournament. Just knowing this unranked newbie was under the training regimen of Koji, generated interest in the teen for those in the know. Not only were the curious onlookers sitting in the bleachers, but in the front row was Melanie, whose unmistakable eyes would follow every point.

Mark cut through his 1950 ranked opponent like butter, creating buzz amongst those viewing the match. His silky smooth style of play, and general lack of sweat disguised his level of effort. His next rival was a teen from the Pennsylvania rated just over 2000. Mark possessed a couple small weaknesses, if one could call them that. He had little interest in developing enigmatic serves. In his book, good players knew how to handle them. He just wanted to get the ball in play without ceding easy returns. The second one surfaced against this kid from Philly, in the form of compassion, and lack of a killer instinct. Whacking balls against expressionless robots, was different than experiencing real emotions on the faces of his opponents.

Koji always said that the player across from you is just as nervous as you are. Some hide it better than others. The younger the player, the more likely they were to reveal their inner feelings. The downcast body language of this mercurial kid from Philly clearly reflected Mark's dominance of him in game one. When Mark crushed Lukas, he drew from the basement player remark and unleased his fury. He had nothing against this kid.

Mark wasn't playing for anything besides some tournament experience and a rating, and his compassionate side surfaced. Early in game two, a couple lucky nets and an edge point reinvigorated and restored confidence to Mark's challenger. Mark found himself down 7-3 in game two. Koji's advice resonated within him, *whatever you undertake, do your best or it is not worth doing. Like Leah with a pencil, use your artistry on the table.* Mark snapped out of his empathetic malaise and dominated the final two games.

The final opponent was the top seed in Mark's event, rated at 2150. He was a thirty something traditional topspin attacker, formally trained, with a coach joined at the hip. Coaches could be found with older players infatuated with the game, and those having the means to afford one. The pair had no idea that the former world champ, and secret half of Mark's coaching team, was within ear shot.

"Serve short, attack on the third ball," the coach whispered to his player, with his hand covering his mouth. Leon chuckled inaudibly. The advice would be impossible to execute, as Mark negated the ineffective strategy, and breezed three games to zero. He dispensed a smidgen of additional latent horsepower to get through the match, at least more than the ping pong club players had witnessed anyway. They had not seen anything close to his best, yet.

Mark moved around with the rest of the students to see Stephanie and Yuan capture third place trophies. Tied at two games each in the final, Lukas was in trouble and couldn't pull out the last game, securing a second place finish, netted him a cash prize as well as the trophy. High fives and hugs ensued from the club members. Mark, Leon, and some of the club members stuck around for the final two players, both ranked over 2600.

Two weeks after the tournament Mark walked into the kitchen and Koji was sitting at the island.

"It's posted," said Koji. "Congratulations on your first rating. Take a look."

"Wow, 2175," said Mark.

"Most kids start well under 1000, and then tournament after tournament they climb the ranks. Some by stairs, and some by escalators. You hopped on the express elevator to the twenty-first floor. Not that you put in any less work, you just showed up on the radar screen out of nowhere. We've got you in the under 2350 in two weeks. Lukas isn't going to play in that one, and you will be eligible for some cash prizes also."

In place of the usual ping pong club meeting Thursday afternoon, Mark booked a ninety minute session at *Mel's*, the iconic retro arcade and eatery in the older part of town. Lukas, now eager to recreate his image, offered his tournament winnings to help pick up the tab. The members all went home first and dropped off their books. Lukas' girlfriend Hannah stopped by the Yamaguchi's to pick up the guys. Mark opened the Yamaguchi's front door in front of Lukas.

"Is that Melanie in the back seat?"

"Dude, I swear I didn't know Hannah was picking her up."

Mark slid into the back seat and was greeted by an infectious smile from his flirtatious pursuer. The surprise of her presence rearranged his stomach a bit, but Mark straddled the line between friendliness and attraction, one he had never had to walk.

Hannah screeched into the parking lot and a neon sign flashed *Mel's Arcade and Pizza.* Most of the nearby businesses were new, but this iconic funhouse stood the test of time. As soon as Mark held the castle-like door open, the bedlam inside provided an audible elixir to his wavering emotions. The clacks, dings, and waka-waka sounds merged with the conversational din. It was just the distraction the doctor ordered. Mark and Melanie exchanged turns at Ms. Pac-Man, the pinballs, and competed in foosball. After the group rotated around the various machines, they gathered at two long tables in the back for pizza. After a round of applause, Mark and Lucas exited into Hannah's car, abuzz from the afternoon bash.

February's tournament was essentially a carbon copy of the one in January, except for the absence of Lukas, and the bump up in competition. Leon sat alone incognito, Koji assisted Scott, and a large contingent of the ping pong club was on hand. Mark, riding his uptick of self-confidence from the success of the arcade outing, rolled along undefeated. There were still other matches going on, and he elected to wait around for the semi- finals and finals of the Open. While he was standing on the far end watching a match, Melanie approached him.

"Scott said it was okay if we went into the party room and played. I didn't bring a paddle. Do you have an extra one I can use?"

"Sure. See that blue sport bag on the stands over there, the one with the three mountain peaks on the front. Take the paddle that's laying on the bottom, the one with the number three on the bottom of the handle."

"Thank you Mark."

Melanie sauntered over to the other side of the building and opened the bag. When moving aside a shirt to find to the paddle, she stumbled across a white headband, adorned with a red logo. Before lifting out the paddle, she slipped the band around her forehead. Melanie was the type who could don any accessory and grace a teen magazine cover. As she walked past a group of highly-ranked Asian players, she indeed got the lengthier stares, and a few clicks from a cell phone camera. They knew who wore that band, but why would she be wearing it? From the other side of the facility, Mark glanced up from the match he was engrossed in, and let out an audible Nooo!

"What's wrong?" asked Yuan.

Struggling for an answer, Mark replied.

"I, I just remembered something."

The red Z with the trailing lightning bolt was undecipherable from a distance, but in front of the stands, it was clear. As Melanie headed towards the party room, Mark saw the group of players huddled together, passing a phone around, with thumbs and forefingers busy enlarging the image. It was too late for Mark to run over to her and ask her to remove it. How petty, Mark thought, not to allow a girl to wear your headband. Of course it would be an easy way to cool things down, and look like a real jerk in the process.

At this point, Mark became nervous about Leon being in the stands. Walking over to him and asking him to leave was not the most subtle move, so Mark reached into his pocket grabbed his phone. Fortunately Leon carried one of the Yamaguchi's spares, and Mark hit him up with a text.

Li. Why don't you walk up a couple blocks to the Starbucks on Grant and grab an Uber home. The app is on the phone so you should be good to go. I'll explain later.

Leon Zeng likely hadn't popped into the minds of any players at the club recently. The fervent fans knew he had disappeared from play, and the headband sighting was bound to stir up some interest. The group of players who saw the headband, would likely pull up some images. Despite Leon's changed appearance, Mark wanted to take no chances.

"Where did you get that Gucci headband?" asked Hannah as they started to rally.

"It was in Mark's bag, so I just decided to be a bit wild."

Scott and Koji were busy with administrative things when Melanie walked by, and now she was out of sight in the party room. All Mark could do was wait things out. When Melanie was done playing, she walked back with the headband in one hand and the paddle in the other. This was not before she had snapped a selfie of herself donning this accessory. She returned the items to Mark's bag, and that did not go unnoticed by the players in the group. Coincidental it was, that the headband belonged to the kid who had emerged out of nowhere, and shredded the 2000 plus competition.

"I hope you didn't mind," said Melanie as her and Hannah sat down besides Mark.

"Mind what?" asked Mark.

"Me putting on that headband. It was pretty silly of me."

"Oh, not at all."

"I think some guys were making comments about me as I walked by. Where did you get it anyway?"

"Don't worry about it. A friend gave it to me."

"Cool."

Mark's picture was taken with his first place trophy, along with a nice check for three hundred dollars. He texted the picture to his parents, and to Leah. Then he was back to his preoccupation with the headband. He pondered, did he keep quiet about the incident, and hope nothing became of it, or did he tell Koji?

Mark watched the Open final and walked over to Koji.

"I told Leon to get an *Uber* home. A girl from the ping pong club borrowed my backup paddle and found the headband Leon gave to me. She put it on, and I think the group of players sitting over there recognized it."

"Hopefully they won't think too much of it. Good move. I know most of those guys. They play on Friday nights. I will keep my ears open for any buzz. They might have some fun tossing out the pictures on social media. Is it real, or is it a hoax? I'll just say the headband is homemade, so don't panic. Most of what you still read on the internet says he is somewhere in China, so I don't think anyone would have reason to believe he's here. Just to be safe, we should keep him away for a while."

"I'm sorry I was careless Mr. Yamaguchi."

"Things happen. Oh, and congratulations. Don't let that overshadow what you have accomplished so far."

Scott didn't need that distraction to enter into his plans, but figured this would fade away with time. Koji had an idea, ran it past Scott, and called Leah at Cornell.

"I need you to do something. I attached some images of Leon's headband. Can you find a plain white one, and duplicate it?"

"Yeah sure Dad. I've got some red fabric paint, dyes, and permanent marker. What's up?"

"Well, the real one made an unexpected appearance at the club."

"Go on Dad."

"One of the girls in the ping pong club got it out of Mark's bag and wore it around, which stirred up some interest, and not the kind we want. So I think I am going to tackle the problem head-on, so to speak."

"Funny. When do you need it?"

"ASAP. Overnight it, so it is here on Wednesday to be safe. That gives you three days. Is that enough?"

"Sure Dad. I'll do my best."

Koji picked up the package on Wednesday afternoon, and in Leah fashion, the band was indistinguishable from the original, at a distance.

Nice job, perfect, texted Koji.

Thanks Dad. It took a few tries. I was having trouble keeping the edges from bleeding out.

Koji told Mark about his idea, and Mark wanted to add his idea to the great headband cover up. Thursday morning, Mark slipped the headband into his paddle case so it would be ready for the ping pong club meeting that afternoon. Mark walked over to Melanie before things got going.

"Hey, I saw your Facebook page and your selfie with the headband on. It looks great, but I think I can make it a little sharper. I was wondering if after the meeting, you could put on the headband and I could make it perfect."

While appearing to keep this fire burning, he was really looking to extinguish another one. When the club broke up, the two of them hung around until everyone had left. Mark pulled out the knockoff, and Melanie slipped it on. In rapid succession, Mark captured six quick images.

"I like the third one," said Mark.

"Me too."

Immediately, Melanie uploaded the new image to her Facebook page. If someone looked carefully at the band, the red was close, but not exact. Also, the edges of the Z and lightning bolt lacked the sharpness of the original. Only a discriminating person, and someone really interested, would be able to discern the difference.

Mark returned the headband to Koji, and they checked Melanie's Facebook page.

"Mission accomplished Mark. Nice work."

"I see what you're saying about the difference," said Koji. "Is somebody really going to look at it that close? Let's see how it goes tomorrow night."

Friday night, Koji strolled into Scott's club, and before he began warming up he slipped on the knockoff. Laughter broke out as Koji mugged everyone with a variety of serious faces. Scott and Skip joined in with the ribbing, making a mockery of the situation.

"Are you the new number one now?" asked one of the players.

"Actually, my daughter made a couple of them. Scott and I were going to wear them as a doubles partners."

When the club closed, Scott, Skip, and Koji gathered in Scott's office.

"I think we diffused that one," said Scott. "If we were quiet, evasive, or sketchy, that might have made those guys dig in for answers, and spread a bunch of rumors."

CHAPTER 18

THE FLASHING LIGHTS

It was late February, and had been gray for a few days. Blue could always be found emanating from Melanie's eyes, which in laser like fashion, melted seventeen year old guys. Lukas continued to be respectful of Mark's relationship with Leah. He refrained from inviting Hannah over to the Yamaguchi's, for fear she would bring Melanie. This weekend, Leah was coming home for the first time this semester, having had her nose buried in the books.

Late Friday afternoon, Leah stepped out of her ride from Cornell lugging her backpack inside the front door. An aromatic blast welcomed her from the seasonal forty five degrees into the warm foyer of her home.

"Hi Mom. What's cooking?"

"Nice to see you too." joked Kate, delivering a big hug. "We're having homemade pan fried noodles and orange chicken. The male contingent is in the usual place."

Leah walked downstairs into the basement to experience a different aroma. Four sweaty guys stopped their play and went over to welcome her.

"No hugs please," she said smiling.

"Okay guys," said Koji. "Let's call it an evening. There is a wonderful meal waiting, and we all need to take showers. So let's keep them short so we can all have hot water."

Finally, everyone gathered around the dining room table. It was one of the most relaxed dinners that everyone had enjoyed since the three young males arrived. Lukas' choir boy behavior following the basement bash had restored calm to the household. Had Leon been implicated and deported, Lukas might as well have committed a capital offense. The incident was now a speed bump in, but it still reverberated, having nearly took down the consortium. The dinner conversation avoided any mention of it.

"So Leon, what's this I hear about you getting a little technology into the food pantry?" Asked Leah.

"Oh, nothing much. I just developed a spreadsheet and small database to make the distribution of goods more efficient. How about you guys and that sensor?"

"Mark and I presented to the company where I work part-time in the summer. They're going to evaluate it."

"How does that work? asked Lukas.

"Well, it's kind of like the Wii, or any other game controller, but the software is intuitive. The chip in the table tennis blade handle communicates to the robot, and based on the location of the paddle, the robot fires the next ball in a location it believes will present the most difficulty to the player."

"Awesome."

The rest of the table conversation moved around to Cornell, Hannah, and Mark's parent's new place in Billings. The group broke up, and late into the evening, everyone turned into their respective bedrooms, except for Leah who went into the studio. She texted Mark.

Meet me in the basement in ten minutes.

Mark walked downstairs and Leah waited in her pajamas, flashlight in hand. "Let's play pinball,"

"In the dark?" asked Mark.

"Yeah. It's really cool. It's totally black, and silent until the lights and sounds of the machine take over."

The back glass and the playfield illuminated simultaneously, casting a mellow light on their two faces.

"Here, stand next to me," said Leah. "Reach around me and play the right flipper."

Leah released the plunger, and the silver ball skidded up the chute into play. Leah reached around Mark with her left arm attempting to reach the left flipper.

"It's in two player mode," said Leah. "I take that to mean two players at the same time. You have to stand more sideways, so I can reach the button."

Mark angled his body while being reigned into the softness of the clingy flannel. Attempting to thwart the gravitational advantage of the machine, Leah wiggled and waggled, taking Mark along for the ride. It was impossible for them to keep their fingers on the flipper buttons without essentially becoming one. Focusing on the ball was equally as problematic. The dance in the dark, accompanied by the percussion of bumpers and bells, continued for fifteen minutes. Suddenly, the flippers stopped working, the ball drained down the middle, and complete silence befell the deep basement.

"You tilted it," said Leah laughing and out of breath.

"I did not. That was you pushing me around."

Leah reached underneath the machine to power it down, and in complete darkness threw her arms around Mark and their lips mated. She reached into her pocket and pulled out the flashlight. In her frolicsome and spell breaking manner, she extended her arm, beamed it between their faces, and spoke with authority.

"Hawthorne Police!"

"Not again," Mark said, and they both laughed.

Mark followed behind Leah's ray of light out the basement and up to the kitchen. As if to further cool things down, she suggested,

"Let's have some ice cream." The pair proceeded to polish off a pint of vanilla with caramel sauce.

The next day Mark Skyped with his parents. Your grades are truly outstanding, said Mrs. Linderman as her as her husband's head also squeezed into the frame of Mark's tablet. How's school outside of the classroom?

I mostly hang around with Leah, Lukas, and the kids from the ping pong club. I went to some basketball games, and volleyball games. Homework, practice, and the club take up a lot of time.

Are you going to come home during spring break?

Leah and I were talking about coming there early in the summer because she wants to go to Yellowstone. Is that Okay?

Sure, sure. Answered both parents together, surprising Mark with their spontaneity and his dad's mellow attitude.

Just let us know, said Mark's mom.

On a rainy Sunday in March, Skip pulled up the Yamaguchi's, and along with Scott dashed to the front porch for cover.

"C'mon in guys. Here's a couple of hand towels." said Mrs. Yamaguchi.

"The stream is roaring by my place," said Scott. "Smells great as usual."

"Koji cooked a large tray of salmon, moist and flaky," she replied.

This was an impromptu assemblage of the people behind Mark, a friendly and casual meeting of the minds. With Lukas tied up for the evening, and Leah just back for spring break, Koji jumped on the opportunity to have the guys over. Lukas was helping out with props for the high school play, which Hannah had a big role in.

Scott had news, and it was easier to talk about plans for Mark when Lukas was absent. When the meal ended, the rain subsided with beams of sunshine brightening up the dining room.

"That salmon was out of this world," said Skip.

"The best," said Scott. "Well I have my state of the union address. First things first, Leah I heard you want to go back with Mark this summer to Montana."

"Yeah, we don't know when."

"That's great. Mark, I was thinking that you can miss the March tournament, and really work extra hard during this break. The weather for the next week looks pretty crappy, so it is a good time to step it up. I think that you can enter the under 2500 competition in April. If that goes well, as we believe it will, you can compete in the Open in May. That may just set off a whole bunch of flashing lights in the table tennis community, but that's an eventuality. So I am thinking June would be a good month for you guys to go."

"Sounds great to me," said Leah.

"So here are the details about the process that will determine the United States representative in Ping Pong Diplomacy II. First, there will be regional trials. The top rated player in the region gets a bye, and the other entrants will compete for the remaining spot. So each of the four regions will send two players to the finals. The great news, is that the Eastern regionals will be held at the Hawthorne Center in November. Not only is that good for me, but we don't have to travel."

"That's great news," said Koji.

"So in 2021, eight players will compete for the one spot in a big round robin February 26th, and 27th. It will be held in Aurora, Illinois outside of Chicago. I also found out, because I am on the Diplomacy committee, I will be allotted ten tickets for the showdown in D.C. The player representing the U.S. will also get ten, so let's keep our fingers crossed."

The evening broke up after large helpings of apple pie and ice cream. Leah was mostly hanging around the house during break. She decided to chip away at her mural, work a few hours at the art store, and hang out with her friend Cara while Mark was practicing. She tapped the keys on her phone.

Hey Cara, do you want to hang out tomorrow. Mark is going to be doing intense practice all day tomorrow, and like all day and evening, every day of break.

Sure. Sounds like the only chance you guys will get to be together is in the basement, in the dark. A little PB in the PJ's.

OMG. Too dangerous.

That was spring break. Sacrifices for all parties. Leah worked more, Mark practiced more, and Lukas practiced less. He would occasionally come downstairs and rally, but with only a couple months left in America, he again immersed himself back into his social his life.

CHAPTER 19

THE ASCENT

The club supporters trickled into the Hawthorne Center and were plentiful as usual, sans Lukas. Melanie was there as usual giving her support, but even with the headband episode, seemed to realize that her and Mark would never be a thing. Heading into this April tournament, Mark was as sharp as he had ever been, with nearly non-stop basement action. He carved through the 2400 players, but next month would be a big step up in class.

"Dude, we never thought someone from Montana could just walk into our club, and be so incredible," said Yuan to Mark, who was holding the first place trophy.

"There's always somebody better, waiting for you," replied Mark.

The decision on Leon's asylum had the potential to drag on a long time. With six months behind him, his work restrictions ended. Leon pulled his bike up the food pantry entrance and locked it, before walking inside.

"I can work now." said Leon to Evelyn with a big smile. "I can make money, but only part-time."

"Congratulations. That means you can eat here, finally. It just so happens, I have a pot of stew. Oh, and if you need a reference for a job, tell them to contact me."

"That would be very kind of you."

A fully sated Leon finished his afternoon of helping Evelyn, and rode up the Yamaguchi's driveway, Koji was outside doing some yardwork.

"Hey Leon. How'd it go today?"

"Great. I'm going to look for some jobs."

Scott was paranoid about Leon having to give out his personal information to get legitimately employed, so he contacted Skip. When Skip wasn't doing Scott's books, or helping him with the club, he did accounting work for other clients. So Skip arranged for Leon to come into his office a few days a week to help out, with of course Scott dolling out the cash under the table.

School was over in two weeks, and the May tournament was this weekend. Lukas did not have an airline ticket back to Albania yet, and he was in no hurry to get back home. Leon really wanted to watch Mark play this Saturday, but Koji and Mark were still leery about him having a presence at Hawthorne Center.

The entire ping pong club was on hand for Saturday's matches. Leah was in the thick of studying for exams and needed to stay at Cornell. A Croatian player ranked just over 2800, and 80th in the world rankings was the top seed in the tournament. A Chinese American player, now living in New York City was the second seed at 2620. Two other out of town players came in north of 2500. Mark, with the artificially low rating of 2475, had never faced this level of competition, except of course in the Yamaguchi's basement.

Mark sliced through his half of the bracket without a loss, raising eyebrows amongst the crowd and competitors. After a 3-0 win in the semi-finals, the stage was set for him to engage the Croatian. A large and vociferous crowd was treated to high level play right from the outset. Mark suffered a hard fought 11-8 loss in game one. His demonstrative, and physically intimidating opponent had an unorthodox set of tools, and used each and every one of them. Combining wide angling shots, with close to the table play, Mark was kept on the defensive.

Patience. He is not giving me time so I am pressing. Mix it up. Koji's voice resonated inside Mark.

Mark took a few deep breaths to slow his pace. *I can play that game too, but with quicker reflexes.* He backed off on his offense and began to pick his spots with some cobra-like backhand strikes. Methodically, he adapted to his lanky opponent's game and grinded out the next four games.

Mark stood atop the platform holding his first place trophy, and a check for the most money he had ever had in his grips, fifteen hundred dollars. He stepped down and his fellow club members surrounded him.

"Mel's is my treat next time, said Mark with a big smile."

After the club cleared, Scott, Skip, Koji, and Mark hung around to restore the facility to its normal configuration.

"You had all the answers after that little stumble," said Scott. "A superb performance like that is going to attract a lot of attention."

Sure enough, a few days later, Scott's office phone rang with the Team US coach on the line.

"I see your young star beat that 2800 ranked player in your house."

"Oh Mark, you mean. He picks up the game so fast. He just self-trained himself in his early years and I was lucky enough to latch on to him. Koji has been working with him to smooth out the edges."

"That's still not a normal arc, and I have seen a lot of players.

Some of these kids rise up pretty fast, but his is hyperbolic. Usually we are able to spot these players at a young age, and they come onboard. It would have been nice to know about him and have him on the team. I suppose now it would be pretty disruptive to the other members. I am disappointed in you for not giving me a heads up. The U.S. team could use some representation like his."

"I swear, I didn't know anything about him until very recently," answered Scott, chuckling at the *come onboard* reference."

The conversation ended, and Scott did nothing to ease the skepticism and suspicions of the coach.

Scott was prepared to catch some flak. As soon as Mark won an Open, the whistles and bells would go off. But that phone call wasn't a lot to deal with, let them squawk. Harboring Mark for his own personal gratification could certainly be called selfish, but not unpatriotic. Scott was totally pro-American. If Mark could pull off the miracle in D.C., Mark was free to do whatever he wanted, including joining Team US. For now, Scott had overwhelming influence and resources. Mark was happy and entrenched, and there was no way he could be extracted from his situation.

Now in late May, Leah was finished with her final exams and Mark was wrapping up the school year. The pair made the travel plans to go to Billings in the middle of June. Lukas was just fine with life in America and still made no moves to return. His dad consistently texted with dates and times for flights, but Lukas was balking. Legally, he could stay until August, a year from his arrival, and his dad was not pleased. Table tennis was everything to him, and he wanted his son back in the Albanian spotlight.

You need to come back to help me at the club, and I would love to see you compete again, texted his dad.

Dad, I just want to hang out here the rest of the time. I may not come back here for a long time.

"Flight attendants prepare for takeoff," squawked out over the cabin intercom. Leah looked out of her window seat and Mark turned her way as they lifted off. After a stop in Denver, Mark's parents were waiting for the pair in the arrival area at Billings International.

"Very nice to meet you Leah," said Carl popping the trunk of Candice's sedan, extending his hand to greet her. "Are you excited about Yellowstone?"

"Definitely, Mr. Linderman."

Candice exited the passenger side and gave Leah a hug before everyone slid back in, just avoiding the bum's rush from security.

Mr. Linderman parked next to his truck in the driveway of their new home, and hit the garage opener.

"Thanks for setting it up Dad."

"I checked the tension, and the height of the net."

After some Chinese carry-out, and conversation, Mark and Leah split out to the garage, fired up an old boom box, and sparred.

"It's hot in here, said Leah."

"Perfect," said Mark.

"You know we're leaving about seven tomorrow morning," said Carl, peeking his head inside.

There's twenty million acres to see in America's first national park, and the four travelers kept their hikes moderate. They chose the

tried and true attractions; Old Faithful, The Brink of the Falls, Mt. Washburn trail. Along the trails, an interesting trend developed. Mr. Linderman and Leah would lag back, engaged in conversation. For stretches the group was two-tiered, Mark and his mom, followed by Carl and Leah. For what the pace setters could detect, the outdoorsman in Carl was connecting to the naturalist in Leah.

The second leg of the trip took them along the John D. Rockefeller Jr. Parkway and into Grand Teton National Park where two more days of sightseeing brought the five day hiatus to a close.

"It's too bad Chinook is so far," said Leah as a Billings city limits sign came into view on the right.

"Six hours," said Carl. "After what you just saw, you really want to see a modest house and a garage in need of paint?"

"Just wanted to see where Mark came from."

"Next time," said Carl.

CHAPTER 20

THE RUMORS

Mark and Leah touched down at LaGuardia and elected to take the train back to Hawthorne. Koji pulled into the parking lot of the Metro station and the pair piled in.

"I could tell from your texts you had a great time," said Koji. "The pictures were spectacular."

"We'll do a show and tell when we get home, said Leah."

Leon and Lukas came downstairs and joined everyone in the kitchen. Mark and Leah scrolled through their pictures and gave accounts of the trip.

"Sounds like everyone had a great time," said Kate.

"Tomorrow," said Koji. "It is back to full practice mode. Lukas you are of course optional. Unfortunately, rumors have been swirling about Leon, so we are going to keep him under tighter wraps for a while. Mark, like Scott said, you could probably take a couple tournaments off because your rating spiked, and you can study for your entrance exams. After a couple more tournaments you should easily qualify for the eastern regional spot in Chicago."

"Was that my fault, I mean about Leon?" asked Mark.

"No, we were wracking our brains, but we don't think it's that."

"If they can't do anything to him legally, why do we have to be so secret about him?" asked Mark.

"We're just being extra careful," said Koji.

"Bummer," said Leah. "I'm going back to work tomorrow at the electronics company." "Lukas, when were you thinking of heading back?"

"Oh, I'll go before I have to. There's so much to do, and I want to stay with Hannah as long as I can."

"Just an FYI," said Koji. "If for some reason you don't go back when you are required, you can no longer stay here."

"Yes Mr. Yamaguchi. I understand."

Mark's time in the upstairs studio paid off as he smashed the ACT in July, and the SAT in August. With Mark around so much, Leah's mural sat idle, but she was heading off to Cornell soon and was anxious to get back at it. Leon's asylum proceedings continued to drag on, while Scott in the meantime, tried to keep the lid on the simmering kettle of rumors. He always had visions of Leon being whisked off his bike on the way to the food pantry or Skip's office, never be seen again. So Kate, or Skip occasionally gave him rides to and from work, or volunteering. Leon loved to bike, but he held his frustrations in check, as the process seemed to be working for him, albeit slowly.

Scott continued withholding his payments, and Jeton refrained from taking action against him. Even though Jeton talked a big game on the phone, he didn't have the backbone to expose Scott. Scott had done a lot for him when it came to the club, and Jeton's anger had waned. Jeton just wanted Lukas back, and was aggravated by his son's reluctance to return. Lukas was a moderating force to his dad, helping him at the club, and keeping him on the straight and narrow. Finally, in late July, Lukas capitulated and headed home, but not before his dad had reverted back to his less responsible ways.

In Albania, a couple of Jeton's playing buddies started hanging around and socialized after the club closed. One of the guys brought in some of his homemade *Raki*, the kind that packs a real punch compared to the stuff found on the store shelf. In one of the late night episodes, the social lubricant induced a session full of venting and bragging.

"Well, my son practices with Leon Zeng, blurted Jeton."

"Really?" asked one of his buddies.

"Yeah." Then he realized what had effortlessly flowed out of his mouth, and back peddled.

"I mean he practiced with him when he played him in Bratislava."

A couple more drinks might have led him right down the self-incriminating road to the secret chamber in the Celery Top table. As he dodged a slew of questions, his evasiveness further piqued the interest of his buddies. The upper echelon of table tennis is not a huge one, and now, information is exchanged at the speed of light.

One week later, Scott got a stinging e-mail. A fellow Chinese official also involved in the planning of Ping Pong Diplomacy wrote:

I am certain that Leon Zeng is living in your vicinity and you are well aware of it. It is very deceiving of you to be such a driving force on the committee, and at the same time be harboring our ex-champion. I request that you hand him over. If you fail to do so, I will initiate measures for us to withdraw from the competitive portion of Ping Pong Diplomacy. That would not look very good for you, causing a diplomatic event to be cancelled because of your underhandedness. An investigation could possibly open up, as to how Mr. Zeng actually entered your country. When you are ready, contact me, and I will give you a place and a person to meet with to arrange his departure.

Scott called Skip and Koji to meet over at his house for a brainstorming session.

"One of the committee members seems pretty certain that Leon Zeng is here. The blockbuster news is that he will take measures to withdraw from the competition unless I hand over Leon. Jeton may have chirped, or somebody took that headband thing seriously. Maybe somebody just recognized him," said Scott.

"They probably have no idea that he is in asylum proceedings," said Skip. "There is nothing they can do, but they don't know that."

"Maybe Jeton told someone that Leon is training someone special."

"They agreed to the fabulous venue, and would look pretty bad if they pulled out.

"So much for diplomacy," said Scott. "I can just wait them out for a few months and see how serious they are."

"Oh, they are extremely serious when it comes to their table tennis. Just like someone I know," added Koji. "All of your dreams could disappear if something is not resolved. All the risk you took, all your work, and a whole bunch of money would go right down the drain."

"If things go public, I wouldn't come out of it looking very good," said Scott.

"To say the least," Skip added.

"It wouldn't look very good for them if it went public," said Koji. "The best player in the world wanting to leave not only their signature sport, but the country too. Maybe it is only one unique individual out of billion, but it isn't a good look for them. That's maybe why they want things done through the back door."

"That sounds plausible," said Scott.

"Koji continued, "Maybe it's just one guy with an agenda. A guy who wants to look like a hero himself. Someone who wants to be known as the person who brings back the national champ. Kind of like someone who wants to create an American table tennis hero."

"Interesting," said Scott. "The Chinese would not look favorably on someone keeping that information to themselves."

"I don't think they would pull anything until the last minute," said Koji. "It would look pretty fishy if all of a sudden they reversed course soon after agreeing to the venue. So things should stay quiet until it gets closer. I will continue the training regimen as if it is absolutely certain that the match will occur."

"I'm going to sit on it a while. If you guys have an inspiration, let me know," said Scott.

CHAPTER 21

◆————————————————◆

THE NEW PRESIDENT

The ultimatum that Scott faced was not going any further than Skip and Koji. Mark and Leon needed to remain oblivious to the communication. Scott's sole interest was having a winner in the competition, but first there needed to be a competition. Scott continued to search for the brainchild that would seal the deal, and from the depths of his deviousness, decided to break the ice with the Chinese without consulting his team members. One afternoon, Scott arranged to pick up Leon from Skip's. During the ride home Scott began softening his star coach.

"Okay, Leon, I just want to give you an update on what is happening," said Scott. "The Chinese are quite certain you are here. By here, I don't mean at the Yamaguchi's, but in the vicinity. I don't think anyone has actually set eyes on you. Don't worry, no mafia type guys are going to swoop you up, but I think that we should keep you under the radar until you get your asylum, and until Ping Pong Diplomacy. That's about seven months, and I wouldn't want anything to get complicated before the event. I completely understand that your asylum application is dragging on, and the frustration with not being able to ride your bike around all the time. But if you could just bear with it for a while longer."

"I understand," said Leon.

The pair arrived in the Yamaguchi's driveway, and Scott turned to Leon.

"I almost forgot. I brought along something that the attorney said had stuck to another page, and never got signed.

Scott reached around between the seats and grabbed a clipboard with two pages attached. It appeared like any other document Leon had seen before, and in actuality it was an exact duplicate. The first page had small print extending all the way down to the bottom. On the blank second page, there were lines at the bottom for Leon's printed name, signed name, and date. Scott simultaneously handed the clipboard and his pen to Leon. Scott held up the first page vertically, and Leon automatically imparted his signature on the second.

"Thanks for the ride," said Leon.

"Never a problem."

Scott returned to his office and began composing his back channel proposition. When he finished, he e-mailed the ice breaker to the Chinese official.

To The Honorary Mr. Ling,

First of all, this is between Leon, you, and myself. We both know, it is in our interests to keep this between ourselves. I have a proposal, which is a compromise to the terms of your request. Of course, this is an admission that Leon is present in this country. In the interest of keeping the competition alive, Leon has agreed to go back to China if your player defeats our top American player in the Ping Pong Diplomacy II competition. If the American player wins, Leon will remain here. I have a document stating the above, which has Leon's signature on it. I realize that it is not legally binding, but it is a gentleman's agreement of the highest order, a diplomatic solution. You know my reputation, I always pay up. When you have decided, you can make a copy of the terms above, sign it, and mail it to the Hawthorne Table Tennis Center. Upon receipt, I will mail you my signed copy.

Sincerely, Scott Kobara

Two days later—

Mr. Kobara,

First of all, although I have no proof, I am disappointed that you were likely involved in the smuggling of Leon Zeng into America. Second, upon comparing his signature to what I have researched, it appears to be a match. So I will take you up on your offer. In the event of our victory in Ping Pong Diplomacy II, we will need to arrange a meeting where we can obtain Mr. Zeng. You should receive a signed copy of the agreement in the mail in the near future.

Sincerely, Mr. Ling

Scott replied,

Mr. Ling,

Thank you for cooperating in a diplomatic manner. I look forward to your correspondence. To further clarify, I can guarantee you, that I myself, personally was not responsible for taking Leon out of your country. Quite honestly, he left on his own volition.

Sincerely, Scott Kobara

Scott was now all in. This was the first time he had not called a meeting before making a decision. If Koji was privy to the deal, the pressure on him could manifest itself in different ways, possibly in the practice sessions. Scott had already piled a ton on his unflappable guru, and didn't want to test his breaking point. So it was business as usual back at the Yamaguchi's.

Scott picked up his cell and called his old partner in crime.

"Jeff?"

"Hey Scott. What's happening?"

"Remember I told you to keep April 10th open. I'd like you to do a little climate control work for me again. You know, make things a bit warmer.

"On a ship?"

"No. The Mead Center in Washington, D.C. Most importantly, there are multiple stages there, and the event is in the Fichandler. It's going to have to be done remotely."

"You mean at home?"

"Anyplace you have access to a computer."

"My expertise is in the onsite computers, the electronics, and the mechanical aspects. I would have to bust through their firewalls to be able to take command of their system. I am well versed in networks, but this is a different animal. I have it up on my screen now. Hmm, a newer facility, so the systems may be more up to date and robust. Then again, it isn't like a financial institution. Who would be interested into cracking into a theater?"

"Here's the deal. Said Scott. It's a table tennis tournament. If my entrant Mark is winning, and you don't have to activate the program, I have ten grand just for your efforts. If you launch the program and Mark loses, I will give you twenty five. If Mark wins, fifty grand."

"That's very generous again. I will investigate."

"Okay. I'll be in touch."

With the November Open coming later this month, Leon and Koji were working extremely hard with Mark. Leon was waiting for asylum. Mark was waiting for his college acceptances, as well as a chance to play in the trials in Chicago.

The American people as a whole had been waiting, but for something much more monumental. Tuesday November 3rd, was upon them. The Yamaguchi family, Mark, and Leon gathered in front of the large flat screen for Election Day 2020. Carl Blansfeld, an Independent, and the ex-governor of the 'Cornhusker State' continued to maintain his slight edge in the polls. With the populace tired of the mainstream parties and their divisiveness, Blansfeld gained momentum deep into the campaign.

He was squeaky clean and internationally savvy. Blansfeld vowed to roll up his sleeves and avoid social media. The down home candidate quipped, *you will find no surprises when you peel back my husk.* He was middle of the road, in the middle of the country, with backing from America's third richest man. Leon's asylum status was still pending, and Leon had more than a casual interest in each of the candidate's stances on immigration.

"You guys have so much election coverage," said Leon.

"No one ever believed that a third party candidate could have a chance of winning here," said Koji. "Of course George Washington was an independent, the first one and the only one. Things have become so polarized, and ripe for a change."

At 12:30 a.m., the polls were still close with no predictions. Everyone crashed, except for Leon, switching channels with his right hand, and grabbing handfuls of popcorn with his left. Two hours later, each major network and cable news channel declared a winner.

At 2:37 a.m. Eastern Standard Time, the results from the final battleground state of Michigan are in, and our projection is that Carl Blansfeld will become the next president of the United States.

The Ping Pong Club grew by another eight members. The bigger it got, the more attention it attracted. Mark managed the growing pains as well as anyone could have. The fun and casual atmosphere still made it a great place for meet ups, as well as those who had a more serious bent to their games. Melanie finally met a newcomer and turned her attention away from Mark. Scott donated two more tables, and the Thursday afternoon session was extended a half hour. It had been five months since the members had seen Mark participate in a tournament, and the newbies had never really seen his full-out capabilities.

Scott purchased a couple new sets of aluminum bleachers for his Hawthorne club. He also popped for t-shirts for the ping pong club that one of the girls had designed. On this first Saturday in November, each member from the ping pong club showed up wearing one. Six players from the club were participating, with Mark of course headlining the action. Scott and Koji had their administrative duties during the tournament, but their preoccupation was the rising star from Montana.

Mark's draw included two players above 2700. In four sweeping matches, Mark propelled himself into the elite company of top American players. He downplayed his dazzling performances, and between matches, provided strong support for the other club participants. Both inside and out of school, Mark's popularity soared.

Scott would always video the final match and post it on his website the next day. Aficionados always enjoyed watching the higher level players battle, but in this tournament, the camera sat atop the tripod, like a rock, doing nothing. Scott's paranoia was pervasive. The absence of video was one less tool the competitors would have to detect any vulnerabilities in Mark's play.

In a week, Mark's rating was posted. He was now the second highest rated player in the United States at 2780. He could now bypass the regional qualifying tournament at Scott's club in February, and go right to the Finals in Chicago. Newspaper articles were already speculating who would represent the United States in the Ping Pong Diplomacy showdown. The meteoric rise of the kid from small town Montana was a growing story. Hawthorne High was now buzzing with the thought that one of their students was a step closer to representing the nation. Mark took it all in stride and planned on hunkering down for the next few months.

Scott stopped over Christmas day to spend time with the Yamaguchi's. He was his usual outgoing self, but kept the conversation light, away from the regionals and Ping Pong Diplomacy. His back door deal, like an invisible gorilla, clung to his back, but Scott hid the stress. Should Mark make it to Washington and falter, the primate would roar publicly.

"Mark, are you guys okay on tables at school?" asked Scott.

"We have eight, and don't have any room for any more, unless we find another room, or maybe the gym."

"How's Cornell, and the table tennis club up there Leah?

"School's hard. I didn't join, but maybe one year. I stopped in and checked it out, they're really good every year.

"What does Skip have you doing Leon?"

"I'm doing administrative stuff, and keeping his PC's running."

Scott moved into the kitchen and schmoozed with Kate and Koji, who as usual put on an incredible spread. After dessert, Leah turned to Mark and Leon.

"Hey guys," said Leah. "Do you want to go downstairs and play some *Eight Ball Deluxe*? Three player mode, the person with the highest score doesn't have to help with the cleanup."

Mark stared at Leah who sported a wry smile.

"We'll play it the conventional way."

Mrs. Yamaguchi overheard Leah's suggestion and interjected.

"Is there a way to play the game we don't know about?"

"We just teamed up on it the last time we played," said Leah, again smiling at Mark.

"You know, you're the expert on that machine. That's no fair deal."

"Alright. Me versus both of them. They can add their scores together."

Leah, in her usual manner, picked off the drop targets, activated the multipliers, and nailed the specials. Her competitors struggled to just keep the ball alive on the playfield.

"No need for a calculator down there," said a smiling Leah as the three turned into the kitchen. "I made it two out of three, but there wasn't a need for a third game. See you guys, have fun."

"You guys just clear off the dishes," said Kate, looking at Mark and Leon. "We'll take over from there."

Two days later, from the upstairs studio, Leah caught a glimpse of the mail truck stopped at the end of their driveway. A two inch layer of snow coated the driveway leading out to the box. Leah slipped on her boots and trudged her way to the street and back, glancing downwards at the envelopes.

"Hey Mark," she called downstairs as she entered the foyer.

"Yeah," he answered, as the energy of the room quickly subsided.

"You have a letter addressed to you. It's from Cornell."

Mark ran up the stairs and Leah handed it to him.

"It looks pretty official. I can hover over your shoulder, or leave you alone," said Leah.

"Stay here, I don't know if I can take it."

After carefully separating the top, he removed the tri-folded letter and his eyes snuck up on the first line.

"Congratulations!"

"Hey Dad. Hey Mom. Mark got the acceptance letter."

After Leah's embrace, Leon followed Koji up the stairs and joined into the celebration.

"I'll text Scott and Skip," said Koji.

Mark called his parents, and once things calmed down, the guys returned downstairs. Koji wrapped up practice early as Mark's mind was adrift, and his intensity was understandably subdued by the magnitude of his acceptance.

Mark, and the other top three ranked players in the country received e-mails with their byes to the regional tournaments, and invitations to the playoff. The four winners of the regional tournaments would meet these four in Chicago. This suited Scott just fine, as Mark would continue to be the enigma he had been since busting onto the scene. It was one less opportunity for the competition to observe him.

The player that Mark beat in the last tournament was the favorite in the Regional, and Mark would likely face him in Chicago. So he didn't need to attend. Leah popped in for the weekend, knowing Mark was free, and they caught an afternoon matinee and dinner.

"Looks like a rematch for you in February Mark." Koji said walking in from the long day at the club. "You should face the fourth seed, but it's bunched pretty close at the top."

CHAPTER 22

THE TOP DOG

The cake on the kitchen island was no store bought one. Mrs. Yamaguchi out did herself. The blue rectangular mass supported a vertical wax shaped paddle in the center, black on one side, red on the other. The number eighteen in white graced each side. White icing lined the perimeter, with *Happy Birthday Mark* scrolled across left side of the cake. A white frosted doughnut hole depicted a ping pong ball on the right half. Koji lit the stem at the top of the paddle and Leah turned out the lights. Scott and Skip were present to join in on the singing, and Mark blew out the candle.

"Only the people get old, but never the song," said Koji.

"Another *Koji-ism*," said Leah.

"Well I just hope his paddle is that hot in Chicago," said Skip.

"Nice sports bag," said Mark, opening up a cardboard box.

"It's from all of us, with a little green on the inside. It holds everything except headbands." joked Scott.

"Ha-ha," said Leah. "I can't believe how the last year flew by."

"So you're not coming along with us to Chicago?" asked Scott.

"No. Dad says you guys are going to be talking about pong and not having fun at night. I think the matches would make me a wreck, and I need to study. Just keep the text updates rolling."

Three days after Mark's birthday, finally the long awaited news arrived. Leon received his Grant of Asylum. The household didn't need another cake, but with such short notice, Kate ran to the bakery, securing one adorned with an American flag. She texted Scott and Skip, and yet another celebration ensued.

To Leon, it was no coincidence that his asylum happened only six weeks into the term of the new president. Outside of Leon, no one was happier about the news than Scott. Legally, it was made things easier for everyone, but Scott would remain vigilant about Leon not flaunting his presence.

Thursday morning was a clear departure day for Scott, Koji and Mark. Skip picked up a cold and delayed his travels until Saturday night. Leah and her mom accompanied the three downtown on the Metro, and then split off for a girl's day in Manhattan. With no complications, the trio eased through security and into their comfortable business class seats. The word economy was absent from Scott's vocabulary. He wanted Mark's legs as fresh as possible, another marginal advantage Mark would have over his coach flying competitors.

A stretch limousine awaited at the arrival level and whisked the team off for their thirty mile ride to Naperville. The trio entered the upscale hotel, located in the downtown of the sprawling western suburb. Scott illuminated the number ten on the elevator panel, and the brass gilded enclosure quietly zipped up to the tenth floor. At the end of the hall, Scott inserted his card, and Koji pushed open the door. Mark entered first and paused for a second, taken aback by openness of the spacious suite, complete with kitchenette, and wall to wall windows on two sides.

"Terrific view. I guess I shouldn't have expected any less," said Koji.

"You know those pro golfers who only hit that little white ball seventy times in four hours. Mark here hits seventy shots in minutes. We may have the top table tennis player in the United States right here. Why should he be relegated to some budget hotel? Guys sit in front of the television watching golfers, but hardly anyone watches table tennis. But that one day in April will bring a lot more eyeballs to the game. You guys decide which of the two bedrooms you want. I'll just sleep out here."

"Leah told me her roommate said there was tons of good food around," said Mark. "Chicago style hot dogs, deep dish pizza, juicy Italian beef and sausage."

"Besides all that stuff, the city has an abundance of exceptional restaurants," said Scott. "But none of that is happening before the event. Koji's going to trek over to Whole Foods to gather up a bounty of fresh sustaining foods. We're not going to take any chances on a restaurant. Maybe he will grant you a special dispensation from your diet afterwards."

"I think he deserves that," said Koji.

"Tomorrow," said Scott. We will walk around the downtown and river walk, go over the players, and watch some video. The facility is open for practice, but we can just lay low, and get there early on Saturday and Sunday."

"This place has everything," said Mark as the trio finished walking along the river walk and entered the main section of downtown."

"It's a big 'burb.' A hundred and fifty thousand or so," said Scott.

Fortunately, Koji employed his culinary wizardry to prepare a large batch of chicken fajitas. Mark's voracious appetite was temporarily quelled, but the plethora of eating establishments still taunted his taste buds.

"Just two more days of torture, and then we can temporarily dial down the stringent diet," said Koji.

"You know I love your cooking Koji, but man," said Mark.

After and evening of taking a last look at the competition, and a game of Yahtzee, it was lights out.

Twenty minutes west of downtown Naperville sat the Vaughn Athletic Center in Aurora. The enormous two hundred twenty five thousand square foot facility was more than enough space for eight players, and its center of the country location was a big plus. Each January it hosts the Aurora Cup tournament, with over three hundred players.

"No *Uber* this time, we're cabbing it," said Scott.

"Low forties, not bad for a late February morning here," said Koji as their cab pulled up.

"Yep. The Vaughn Center," Scott barked out to the cabbie as the three slid in.

The zippy ride concluded at the mega center. *Tame* by New York City standards, thought Mark. The three entered the lobby and turned into the main gymnasium. Eight blue tables seemed lost in the vast space bounded by an upper indoor track. A number of umpires and officials, scurried around while players and their coaches checked in at the main station. Four tables were dedicated for competition with umpire stations on each side, in line with the net. Further behind them were a set of portable bleachers. Far removed from the competition area, were the other four tables, designated for warmup and practice.

"Hey Scott, hey Koji, long time no see. Said Bruce Yung, an excellent player and coach of the sixth seed hailing from the West. "So this is the young phenomena, eh. He's quite the buzz around here."

"You'll have to make it back up to the club sometime," said Scott.

"Hello Al," said Scott to the Team US coach bearing a deadpan look on his face.

"Hello," answered Al, in an obligatory tone.

Mark completed his sign in and headed over to warm up with

Koji. After forty five minutes the referee picked up his microphone and a click echoed throughout the building.

"Ladies and Gentlemen. Welcome to a unique and prestigious venue. The top eight players in the United States are gathered here to compete for an esteemed honor. The winner of this competition will represent this country in the fiftieth anniversary of Ping Pong Diplomacy against the People's Republic of China. All players will play each other in a best four out of seven game format. Four matches will be played today, and three tomorrow. The player with the best overall record will be declared the winner. If there is a tie, there will be a playoff. Here are the initial matchups and table assignments."

"Okay Mark," said Koji. "This is your new garage."

Mark removed his warmups and stepped over the official barriers delineating the playing arena for table number three. The two umpires took their positions. Koji was one to avoid coaching conversations during the match, and just took up a seat next to Scott on the bottom plank. Open to the public, a number of local players filed in to witness the play of the elite eight. This particular set of bleachers attracted the greatest number of onlookers. As Mark began to warm up with his opponent, the seventh seed, his eyes caught two people walking over to the bleachers.

Mr. and Mrs. Linderman had never seen their son in a real competition against humans, and were quite struck by the professional nature of the setting. Officials and umpires donned jackets and ties. Laptops on the scorer's table would stream the results to a large information board.

"See Carl, I had that mom's intuition that table tennis would somehow work out for him."

The Yellowstone trip paid unmeasurable dividends. Leah's trifecta of intelligence, looks, and personality softened up Mark's da

d. Mark was riding on this jet stream of affirmation.

"Hello again, said Mark's mom as Scott and Koji stood up to shake hands.

"You made it," said Koji.

"Yeah barely. No Leah?" asked Mr. Linderman.

"No." Answered Scott. "She knew it would be all business, and didn't want to be a distraction."

Mark's parents took up seats directly behind Scott and Koji, and play was ready to begin. Mark received the first serve, and it was game on. Right from the start, the spectators were treated with Mark's synchronous blend of grace, execution, and composure. There were no outbursts or fist pumps, just focus. Mark rolled along with a 4-0 victory. Never before had Mark's parents heard passionate applause for their son.

"I didn't think you guys were going to make it," said Mark as the group moved outside the playing area and into the main corridor.

"We had some delays," said Mark's mom.

"You were amazing," said Mark's dad. "You've made such a remarkable transition from our garage to this big time setting."

"Thanks, Dad."

Through the mid-morning and early afternoon, Mark rolled through his next three opponents. He suffered a first game loss against the number four seed, but he'd been through that before. At this level, the game is one of millimeters, and the difference between skill level narrows. Balls drop over the net, and hit the edges on key points. A game win is a major confidence booster for an underdog, but Mark quickly got back on track in that match, extinguishing any hopes of an upset with a 4-1 victory.

"Do you guys want to go get some dinner tonight?" asked Mr. Linderman.

"We're on the Koji diet for one more day," said Scott. "But if you guys want to come up to the suite and hang out for a while that would be great."

After an early dinner in downtown Naperville, Mr. and Mrs. Linderman took Scott up on the offer and walked up to the luxury accommodations.

"First class," said Mr. Linderman as they sat down. "Look, we just want to thank you for all your efforts and dedication, as well as your generosity. Admittedly, I wasn't too pleased with the events that first transpired, but new worlds have opened up for Mark, as well as us. You never know where my sister-in-law's adventures are going to lead to. I never could have guessed this."

"Well thanks," said Scott. "Our work, and especially your son's work is not over yet. Tomorrow he has three matches, including the final one against the number one seed. The ball can take some unlucky paths sometimes, so we must not get ahead of ourselves. What time is your flight tomorrow?"

"Eight o'clock."

"Well, the tournament should be over at about three. There might be time for an early, dare I say, celebration dinner. We're going to head out Monday morning."

Sunday morning, Scott, Koji, and Mark enjoyed another big breakfast and cabbed it to Aurora. Skip left from his separate room, and grabbed an *Uber*. A larger audience and media presence gathered inside the Vaughn Center on this second and decisive day. Skip greeted the other two members of the consortium and deliberately refrained from shaking hands.

"You made it," said Scott.

"Yeah. I'm doing a lot better. I don't think I'm contagious, and hopefully I will engage in a lot of handshakes later."

The three took up seats alongside each other with Mark's parents behind them. The only pre-match advice that Koji gave Mark, was don't take anyone lightly. In predictable fashion, Mark rolled through the eighth seed. The fifth seed was a crafty thirty year old player of Romanian heritage named Anton. Koji warned

Mark about this guy who occasionally upset higher rated international players. Anton was the only competitor to use anti-spin rubber on one side to neutralize his opponents spin. Koji maintained a collection of paddles with specialty rubbers, ones with anti-spin and pips out, along with some hard bats. He developed and adeptness for using all of them, and gave Mark a feel for their unique characteristics.

Mark started out with a more cautious and defensive posture as he got acclimated to the veteran's deceptive shots. With patience and discipline, Mark gradually turned more aggressive. After losing game three, he established his dominance in the next two, and was on to the final. Forty five minutes now stood between Mark, and the lone player in the event rated above 2800. Mark's mom ventured outside into the cool March air to compose herself, and muster up enough strength to endure the final.

The umpires and officials folded up the other tables, moved the barriers, and arranged a couple more portable bleachers on each side of the final table. The stage was now set as the number of spectators grew to its highest level so far. The tournament director lifted the microphone from its stand.

"Ladies and gentlemen. The final match is upon us, and it will determine the United States representative in Ping Pong Diplomacy II. Both players are coming into the match with six wins, and no losses. On my left is the second seed and Eastern representative Mark Linderman. On my right is the number one seed and Western representative Faiyaz Burman. These are the youngest pair of players to ever occupy the number one and number two rankings in the United States. There will be a five minute warmup period. Good luck gentlemen."

Faiyaz was currently the top United States Olympic representative. He followed the lines of the typical prodigy, hitting balls with his dad in the basement when he could hardly peer over the table. His parents though, were laid back, and never pushy. Faiyaz was just this extremely talented eighteen year old, with a happy go lucky attitude. In fact, he could almost appear lackadaisical before delivering the kill. Koji had cautioned Mark about this, while going over the video of him.

Being put under this magnifying glass, and under the eye of the large crowd, gave Mark a bit of nerves for the first time. Scott's tournaments had their usual gathering of interested onlookers, but nothing like this. After the obligatory paddle inspection by the umpires, and the warmup, play was ready to begin.

Sure enough, right out of the blocks Mark was surprised by a couple of snap backhands. Despite Koji's warnings, Faiyaz's casual demeanor caught Mark with his guard down, Mark had now touched the hot stove, and paid the price. To add insult to injury, Faiyaz led 11-10 in game one when his push clipped the net, and agonizingly dropped on Mark's side. Faiyaz raised his hand to Mark, a common acknowledgement of a lucky break. This gesture of sportsmanship didn't change the situation; Mark was down one game to zero. Faiyaz approached his chair, and conferred with his coach. Mark swigged his water bottle, placed it next to his chair, and quickly ran in place to keep warm.

"Maybe you should go down and give him a shot of confidence," said Scott to Koji.

"You know I never do that. He would know I was carrying your apprehension with me, and he doesn't need that. Staying pat, is a vote of confidence."

Mark possessed all the finesse that Faiyaz was exhibiting, and then some. He just had to mentally unlock it. The abruptness of the net ball acted like a splash of cold water to Mark's face. It was a wake-up call, snapping him out of the temporary spell that was cast upon his game. He flashed back to his garage, Leah, and the positive atmosphere of the Ping Pong Club.

With that mental refresh, the onslaught began. The years in the garage, and the eighteen months of collaborative preparation began to culminate. With a raucous crowd celebrating the mastery, Mark unleashed the potential that Scott recognized aboard The Ping. In the final point of the fifth game, Mark delivered the match winner, a precisely placed a backhand slam to the deepest part of Faiyaz's left corner. The fans erupted. Mark's team and parents hugged, while exuberant cheers echoed above the clapping. Mark shook hands with the umpires and the tournament officials, before more congratulatory chaos ensued in the Linderman camp. Scott immediately texted Leah, her mom, and Leon. Candice texted Kathy. Mark's final winning smash would propel him into the history books, win or lose in Washington, D.C.

The Team US president and head coach approached Mark and Scott.

"Congratulations. That was one meteoric rise to the top," said the president shaking their hands.

"Thank you," said Scott. "Well Mark's not unique in that regard. Look at that Olympic ice skater in the suburbs north of here who got the Bronze medal. Hardly anyone knew anything about her until she competed."

Scott always seemed to have a comeback. As the crowd thinned out he suggested to Mark's parents.

"I think we have time for some Chicago style deep dish pizza, before you guys need to head out. I'll call ahead to have it ready when we get there."

An oversized white van cab pulled up and the half dozen out of towners piled in. The cab sped away and after ten minutes Scott barked out to the driver.

"Pull over. Over there at that stand. Leave the meter running."

The cab pulled into a small parking lot next to a small building with red and yellow signage. The cab with Mark's parents followed them into the lot.

"Everybody out," said Scott."

As they walked inside Scott lead the parade, "One, everything except relish and hot peppers,"

"Put peppers on mine," Mark called out next. "I like things hot."

The remaining four adults opted for the milder versions. Side by side, all six sat along a narrow counter, butted against a long window facing the street. Their elbows straddled the paper lined baskets, and condiments rained down with each bite.

"Chicago style," said Scott. "Onion, tomato, pickles, mustard, celery salt. Definitely no ketchup, that's a sin in these parts. Consider this your salad ahead of the pizza."

With mustard splotched on his lips, a garbled "killer" found its way out of Mark's overflowing mouth. Skip hustled outside and clicked off a few pictures of the indulging lineup.

"We really started the celebration in high style," joked Koji. "A bunch of hot dogs, but I can't argue, they are incredible."

The six finished their appetizers, hopped in the van, and the aroma of their main course greeted them as they entered the quintessential Chicago pizza establishment. A hefty wooden table in the rear of the restaurant awaited the out of towners. Within minutes, a couple of thick pies landed in the center of the table.

"Which one is half kale?" asked Koji.

"Very funny," said Scott.

"Heavenly," said Skip after a few bites.

"This is the best," said Mark. "I'd like to take the leftovers."

"I saw a sign saying you can have them shipped frozen," said Scott. "Let's just do that some time."

After a round of hugs outside the restaurant, Mark's parents grabbed a cab to O'Hare.

"See you guys in April," exclaimed Mark's mom.

CHAPTER 23

THE CHALLENGER

Mark and Koji walked into the Yamaguchi's and received a warm welcome from Leah, her mom, and Leon.

"You did it, you did it!" Exclaimed Mrs. Yamaguchi. "Sit down, tell us about the trip."

The family sat around the kitchen island until midnight basking in Mark's accomplishment, and discussing D.C. The next day, Scott was anxious to start organizing the trip. Skip sat in his office in the Hawthorne center and Scott walked in. Scott began to rattle off his checklist.

"Okay, the team is going to take the train. That will include Mrs. Yamaguchi, Leah, and Leon. Take care of the Linderman's airfare and hotel, including Kathy. From what I gathered, things are okay between her and Mark's parents now. Set them up for business class on all their connections. Check to see if anything else huge is going on in D.C. that week. Get Mark another backup paddle that you won't let out of your sight. Make sure Doug can help out and do a marathon here over the three days."

When Mark walked into the main hallway at Hawthorne High, there was a huge banner strung in the main entrance area with DC written on paddles with a big *Congratulations Mark* painted across it in large letters. He was at least temporarily the big man on campus, and students would lock eyes on his as they passed.

Another banner with all the member's signatures greeted Mark as he entered the ping pong club. Reproduced articles about the original Ping Pong Diplomacy were posted around the walls of the room. Some of the student's parents were not alive when it took place, and Mark's accomplishments cultivated interest in the historic event. There were more than members waiting in the club. The Principal, Athletic Director, and some additional faculty members mingled among the students. After a few minutes, the Principal took command of the moment.

"Step up here next to me Mark. This is a significant achievement for you, and we are privileged to have you representing our school. We know you have put in a ton of work. You are a model student, and exemplary Ping Pong Club president. The students and faculty congratulate you, and give you all of our support in the fiftieth anniversary of Ping Pong Diplomacy."

A large round of applause ensued and Mark signaled that he had something to add.

"I have some good news and some bad news. Let me start with the bad news. Not everyone will be able to attend Ping Pong Diplomacy. The good news, is that I do have eight tickets available for the club members. Scott Kobara will generously take care of everyone's transportation and two hotel suites. There will be one for the guys, and one for the girls. Oh, and I am only the messenger, but there will be a parent in each of the rooms. I have been told, that President Blansfeld, and other dignitaries will likely be attending. A week from this Thursday, we will have a drawing for the tickets here."

Not a lot of playing got done during the lunch hour. Students gathered around Mark while the Principle soaked up the positive atmosphere. The editor and photographer from the school newspaper interviewed Mark and took some shots. The local as well as the national media was having a wonderful time with the Cinderella story from small town Montana. Mark had conducted a half dozen interviews with various media names, and the table tennis sites were buzzing. It was great fodder for the writers, the kid from nowhere now opposing the mighty Chinese. Mark wove his way through the questions, avoiding getting tripped and mentioning The Ping or Leon. He continued to be a bit hazy about the actual timeline of events. But who would ever suspect him of hopping onboard a ship, and then secretly training with the greatest player of all time.

Outside, after school, a local reporter collared Mark.

"Mark. Just a couple questions. You flew under the radar as a kid. But just how did you and Scott Kobara hook up?"

"Well, I sought him out," said Mark. I wasn't rated, but I was able to capture his attention with my play."

"Do you intend to get on the Olympic Team, and have they pursued you?

"I'm just taking it one step at a time right now, which includes getting back to studying and practicing."

Now that Mark's background was publicized, he was getting contacted by robot manufacturers. Back at the house, he conferred with Koji.

"Koji. What do I do? I've got a couple table tennis robot makers wanting to meet, and maybe have me endorse their products."

"I would wait. If you and Leah can perfect the intuitive software, then you will really have leverage. Win or lose in D.C., those offers will still be there, and for other products as well, believe me. By the way, you never mentioned the brand you were using to anyone, did you?

"No."

"Do you have pictures that show the robots you used?"

"Oh yeah. I fooled around with some selfies, and I'm sure the robots are visible behind me. I have videos too. They're on my thumb drives, and the cloud."

Back in Albania, Jeton was happy now that Lukas was back playing and helping out at his club. His anger waned, he stopped drinking, and never pressed Scott for any more money. When it came to the showdown in D.C., he and his son would firmly be in Mark's camp.

Team US officials expected all along that one of their own players would be representing the U.S. in Washington. They had no axe to grind with Mark, Scott was the villain. They would have loved to dig up some dirt on him, but it was risky. Team US had a stellar reputation, but if anyone had the drive and resources to turn the microscope back in their direction, it was Scott. So officials outwardly praised Scott, Koji, and Mark, while stewing in the process.

Thursday afternoon, Mark rolled into the ping pong club and set a large box on a folding table.

"Okay, listen up everyone," said Mark. He removed a bowl, a canister vacuum, and an empty oversized clear jar with a duct taped lid.

"I assume all thirty two of you are here, but let's do a quick headcount."

"Thirty two," said Yuan.

"Everyone reach into the bowl and grab a folded sticky note. Girls take the orange ones. There will be a number inside. I have eighteen orange balls for the girls and fourteen white balls for the guys. I will pull four of each color."

Mark attached the hose to the reverse flow outlet of the vacuum and plugged it in. He placed the end of the hose onto the cutout top of the clear jar.

"Ready?"

Mark flipped the switch and the force of the air chaotically circulated the balls within the confined space.

"Okay, hang on, it's not *Powerball* ready, but let's just call it our *Big Game* drawing.

Mark relocated the hose onto the suction end of the canister, and placed it over the lid. He turned on the machine and a ball immediately was sucked upwards, clogging the end of the round tapered nozzle. He gripped the ball, flipped off the switch, and rotated it.

"Eleven orange!" He called out.

"Woo-hoo!" Yelled Erin, elevating her arms into the air and dancing in place.

Mark wrote down her name and repeated the process, garnering seven more students. Mark emptied the container, it was time for the parents to be drawn. He placed the eight winning balls inside, fired up his apparatus, and after the gyrations, Mark plucked an orange number six from the canister.

"Erin!" "Your parents are going. Congratulations. I wish I had tickets for everyone. Oh, and some information for the winners. There might be background checks, because the President, some of his staff, and foreign dignitaries are going to be there. That's it. So there's some time left to play."

The Chinese remained quiet over the last couple months, but were required by the Ping Pong Diplomacy rules, to announce their entrant on March 1st. This was conveniently right after the United States final, giving them the advantage of seeing who the American representative would be. They had at least three equally adept contenders to choose from. Contrary to the American playoff system, they decided to choose the player they believed would present the greatest difficulty to the American competitor. Throughout their decades of dominance though, it usually never mattered who they threw out there.

China's choice of players was twenty-four year old Kai Meng. Currently, he was ranked second in the world behind another Chinese player, who he would occasionally beat. Koji turned to the biggest insider of all to get the scoop.

"You were right Leon, they chose Kai."

"Yeah, I played with him, and was able to handle him. He is a non-conformist, and when I disappeared, they needed him even more. He was so popular and kept winning, but made the officials so angry with his casual attitude and lack of work ethic. The public loves him because of his rebellious nature. If he was kicked off the team, I think there would be a revolution. So Kai feeds off of the populace."

"So why do you think they chose him for this event? He sounds risky."

"They know when he really tries, he is the best, at least now anyway. There might be a lot of pressure because he is such a people favorite. Maybe they are going to greatly reward him. Also his style is probably the most frustrating. He will test a player's patience."

"How well did you know him?"

"You got to know the guys on the team pretty well spending so much time with them. Especially the top players. I never mentioned anything to anyone about wanting to quit."

"Okay. We have a little more than a month to prepare for him."

"He's pretty rock solid in all aspects, but I'll try to mimic his style as much as possible in practice."

CHAPTER 24

THE ASSEMBLAGE

Leah's mural was complete except for one thing, Mark's opponent. She found some older online images from a tournament in Frankfort and obtained a reasonable shot of Kai Meng. Friday night, the first weekend in March, Leah snuck into the house and met Koji in the basement. She carefully unrolled the mural and spread it across the ping pong table.

"Spectacular as always," said Koji.

Across from the canyon scene, Leah and her dad hung the inspirational piece. The following morning after a big breakfast, Leah and her mom slipped downstairs ahead of the guys. Koji led Leon and Mark downstairs, flipping the lights before the trio entered their practice area. Mark did a quick double take, and then fixated on the scene. Leah and her mom stepped into the space.

"It feels like I'm there," said Mark. "Incredible."

"And we all will be," said Leah.

Leah depicted the crowd in a sketchy, less focused manner than Mark and Kai, who were sharply drawn, fully engaged in action, across the table from each other.

"No need for a *Koji-ism*," said Koji. "Two experts competing on the big stage. Awesome."

"I'm glad I'm here and not Kai," said Leon. I don't think I could deal with all that pressure."

"Thanks a lot Leon," said Mark.

"No, I mean, I would be expected to win. I never got to experience being the underdog."

"Well every day is going to be *Kai day* from here on out," joked Koji.

"Bad pun Dad," said Leah.

Back at the Hawthorne Center, Scott's phone rang.

"Hey Jeff. What's going on?"

"You know I was reading about Ping Pong Diplomacy II. The President as well as a whole bunch of important people are going to be there."

"There certainly will be a ton of security there, but that doesn't mean their computer systems are going to be any more secure."

"No, I mean like, if I am caught, they might think I was trying to direct something really malicious towards them. Maybe like carbon monoxide poisoning, or wanting to kill a foreign dignitary with a heart condition. What do I say if I am caught? If I stay quiet they will think I am some kind of terrorist, and I will spend the rest of my life in prison. If I tell them I did it to help the American win, they will think I'm crazy. If I drag you in—me, or both of us would be notorious on a national level, international for that matter."

"Wow. You're extrapolating this into a grandiose case of paranoia. It's just heating and air conditioning. No one gets hurt.

The President and everyone sweats a little more. He's probably gotten used to that already."

"Yeah but my feet are getting cold."

"Very funny. You won't even be there. You'll be at home with the TV on, watching my superstar with your program ready to launch only if needed. If Mark is handling the Chinese player, you don't have to do anything, and you still get paid. If he is getting beat, then you turn up the heat. Remember, this is your judgement call because they won't allow cell phones to be out during the match."

"I guess. But there is going to be a small digital footprint."

"Like I said, no one has a reason to be looking for one. You just turn on the toaster, and if need be, I'll sweep up the trail of crumbs with some greenbacks. Just think of the intrigue of this. An international event, and only you and I know why something is happening. I tell you what, I'll double the ante for all the stages."

"Alright."

"Oh, and make sure you can switch to an antenna if you lose your cable." As Scott hung up, Skip walked in.

"Who was that?"

"Some contractor."

"No correspondence from the Chinese?

"No. I guess that means all systems are go."

"Maybe they really don't want to look bad, but will put the pressure on afterwards."

"Hard to guess."

"Here's a big envelope from Fed X, and a package from UPS. The envelope is official looking, maybe it's the tickets."

Scott carefully cut open the top of the envelope. One smaller envelope housed the tickets. Two pages of strict rules and regulations accompanied them.

"Very official looking, hologram and all, with each person's name on them. There's nine. Koji, Kate, Leah, Leon, Candice, Carl,

Kathy, you, and me. Everyone had a role in Mark being here or taking care of him. The tenth ticket would have gone to an outsider, so I just stuck with the core group. Stick around for a minute while I open this box."

Carefully cutting the top of the box, Scott dug into the bubble wrap and pulled out one of many individually wrapped wooden boxes.

"Just elegant. Said Skip. "What kind of wood is that?"

"Rosewood. Open it."

Engraved on top of the smooth and richly stained box were the words Ping Pong Diplomacy 2, with April 10th 2021 directly underneath. Skip flipped open the cover and two handcrafted wooden pens were nestled in their slots. One dark, one light, with PPD II 2021 engraved on the top portion.

"The diplomacy committee suggested that Mark and the Chinese player exchange gifts, like in 1971. Something hand crafted in each of the countries."

"Wow. What kind of woods are these?"

Well the darker one is American Cherry, and the lighter one is Celery Top Pine.

"You devil!"

"You know I like to give back. The wood that was used to snatch the greatest Chinese player is now being returned back to them in the form of a writing instrument. Beautiful irony, isn't it?"

"Only you could come up with something like that. There's still a slight scent. They came from Maine?"

"Yeah, the smell is a lingering good memory. I found the craftsperson online. There's a lot of people that do this, but this guy kind of stood out for me. I ordered a dozen. Each member of our team will get one as well."

"Do you want them in the safe for now?"

"Absolutely."

As Mark walked into the ping pong club Yuan intercepted him.

"Dude!" "You're huge! *ABC* live coverage just two weeks from Saturday. The school is going to have a special viewing event in the auditorium."

"You don't have to tell me."

"Yeah, there's a reporter over there waiting, and there's non-members in here checking out all the buzz. People want to see you play now that you're famous."

"Anything that gets more people playing is a good thing."

"I can't argue with that," said Yuan.

"Maybe I'll miss a couple of meetings and come back a week from Tuesday at lunchtime. Things are a little crazy around here. We'll be leaving the Thursday before the event anyway."

Mark comfortably got through the interview, and engaged in some higher level play with Yuan to appease the outsiders. Tuesday, four days before the event, Mark's parents arrived at the Hawthorne Metro station.

"Great to see you again," said Koji. "You guys are still heading over to the high school, right?"

"Yeah. Mark just texted us," replied Candice.

"I'll wait for you outside. This is your time," said Koji.

Mark was waiting inside the main entrance where his parents entered, and they stopped to marvel at the huge banner spanning the lobby. School had been out for a half hour, but students were still milling around with activities in progress. The principal received the call that they were heading to his office and he greeted them part way up the hall.

"Welcome to Hawthorne High. A pleasure to meet you two. You have a fine citizen here in Mark. These are extraordinary times around here now. So much electricity. Usually it is like this before a big football game, or Homecoming week. But I've never seen the school get behind an individual like this."

"He's always been a self-starter," said his mom. "Maintenance free, so to speak."

"Believe me, I know you set a fine example for him the first sixteen years of his life, and he is thriving in this unique situation. The Yamaguchi's are thrilled to have him, and he's gotten himself into Cornell. It is unprecedented, and an honor to have a current student represent the school on the world stage. We are blessed to have him here and grateful for your sacrifices. Let's take a walk. It means a lot to him that you could make it. Of course I believe you will be back again for graduation."

"There's my AP Physics class," said Mark, as the four strolled down the hallway. "That's obviously the gymnasium, and *ta da*, the ping pong club room."

"The club has grown and has achieved a much higher profile thanks to Mark," said Mr. Price.

"Another banner," commented Mr. Linderman.

After the brief orientation, Mr. Price slowly walked the three back to the main lobby, shook their hands, and spoke.

"It was wonderful meeting you two. Safe travels, and Mark, the best of luck from all the students and faculty. We'll be cheering in the auditorium."

The trio hopped back into Koji's car, and back at the house Kate greeted them at the door.

"It is wonderful to finally meet you in person Mrs. Yamaguchi," said Mr. Linderman.

"I've been looking forward to it as well."

"Thanks for everything you have done for Mark," said Carl.

"Oh, he was already polished when he got here. We just give him the basics and he is self-driving. Such a pleasure."

"That is so nice of you. Is Leah at school?"

"Yes. She is going to attend her classes tomorrow, and then head out."

"This is Li, our co-coach," said Koji. He is working towards his citizenship."

"My pleasure," said Leon, as he gave Candice a hug, and Carl a firm handshake.

"Kathy should be arriving in an hour or so," said Candice.

"Koji's had some pork slow cooking all day, so dinner will be ready when she gets here," said Kate. I've got a couple big casseroles made for tomorrow, so we can just focus on getting ready. Also, Scott and Skip are coming over, and we all will go over the itinerary. I'll show you guys the guest arrangements. We've had to shift things around to accommodate everyone."

Once the Lindermans were settled, Mark and his parents joined Leon and Koji on the back patio. Kate remained in the kitchen finishing up the side dishes.

"Li has really taken Mark up to new heights," said Koji.

"Mark told us what an excellent player you are and how you have helped him," said Carl.

"Thank you."

"Li's welcome here as long as he wants to stay," said Koji. "But I think he is chomping to go out and find his way. He already volunteers, and has a part-time job. He will make a lot of connections inside and outside of table tennis."

"If he leaves, you will have a huge empty nest," said Candice.

"Yeah. It got a little crazy around here, but I will miss it. Don't mention that to my wife. She will get all emotional."

"Yeah, So Mark, how have the last couple weeks been?" asked his mom.

"Pretty wild. I did interviews for some local stations, and you saw the articles in the national newspapers. I got a big sendoff at the club, and from a lot of students I didn't really know. It was kind of overwhelming.

"I cut out and saved a bunch of those articles. I've got duplicates on my desk." said Koji.

While Carl and Koji were engaged in conversation ranging from Koji's playing days to Carl's life in Montana, Candice's phone buzzed with a text from Kathy.

I'm at the Metro station. How's Carl?

Don't worry. He's as mellow as I have ever seen him, and he seems to be hitting it off with the Yamaguchi's. We'll be over there shortly.

"Koji. Kathy's in. I'll ride over there with you," said Candice.

After the brief round trip, Kathy entered the crowded kitchen first.

"Welcome again," said Kate. "Set your stuff down. Dinner's ready."

"Just like old times," said Kathy, as the group seated themselves around the dining room table. "Looks delicious as always. This alone is worth the trip, and so much is yet to come."

"Thank you. These are exciting times at the house right now, and I am glad we can all share in it," added Koji.

Leah caught a ride back home Wednesday, mid-afternoon. The Lindermans and Kathy piled into the grandpa-mobile, and Leah took the family out for a quick tour of the vicinity.

"That's where Scott lives," said Leah. It's set back pretty far, and when the trees are filled out it is really obscured."

"Pretty impressive." Replied Carl. "Candice told me how forested it was around here, but I couldn't imagine it looking at the map with all the sprawling development."

"We'll take a drive into Whippoorwill Park, one of my favorite places, especially when the stream is rushing." There's a lot of parks, preserves, and lakes around this area," said Leah.

"They haven't seen Scott's club," said Mark.

"Good idea."

The group completed their short ride from the park and arrived at the Hawthorne Table Tennis facility.

"It looks state of the art," said Carl passing through the lobby and into the playing area. "I never would have guessed that there were facilities like this dedicated to the sport."

"They're all over the world, but this is one of the best," said Mark. "Scott has visited a bunch of them. I would like to do that too."

"We should get back because dinner is going to be early," suggested Leah.

Right after the five arrived back home, Skip and Scott pulled up. There was a nervous giddiness in the household. The countdown was on. In three days, the table tennis community would be experiencing their version of the Super Bowl.

"What a great day," said Scott. "And it smells incredible in here."

"Chicken Tortilla Casserole," said Koji.

Scott's huge burning desire to defeat the Chinese had affected many. He expended a ton of resources to get to this point. People who would normally not engage in illegal activities, smuggled, blackmailed, and sabotaged. Hacking was still on the agenda, and right under the new President's nose. For the last two years, all Mark did was hit balls; all Scott did was dupe. The team was flying high on this magic carpet with Scott at the helm. It was cruising on a jet stream of deception. The surface was clean, and the dirt clung to the underside.

Scott had raised the stakes to a level where enjoying the ride to the top was difficult for him. Getting there was certainly not half the fun. His reputation, and possibly his future were literally in the hands of an eighteen year old. Outwardly, he laughed and told jokes on the eve of the departure, while indulging in the generous offerings of the Yamaguchi's. He and Koji kept the atmosphere light as the late afternoon meal wrapped up. When the table was cleared, he stood up from his end seat at the table, leaned on the back of a chair and began.

"This is a great kickoff to a three day celebration of all of our hard work. Thank you Kate and Koji for another outstanding meal. Tomorrow morning, I have a guy picking us up here in a ten seater van to take us over to the Metro. From there we will have about forty five minutes to Grand Central. I understand we all have nice rolling suitcases so we will take a leisurely walk over to Penn Central for the Amtrak. Carl, you will get a quick taste of the Big Apple. It will be about three and one half hours to D.C. There is going to be a personal security detail on the Metro car, and the Amtrak car we are riding in."

"Probably just plain clothes people," said Koji. They don't want anything to go wrong with all the planning involved, and dignitaries travelling seven thousand miles."

"We won't know who they are, but they will know who we are," said Scott. "Now for the awesome stuff. We are all going to go to the White House Friday morning for a quick photo op and meet and greet. I have us all cleared for a tour of The Capitol. We will be transported over there. The Lindermans, Kathy, and I will then attend a luncheon and small ceremony back at the White House with the Chinese dignitaries. You guys in the meantime can take the trolley around the National Mall, hit the Smithsonian museums, and the monuments. We'll meet up with you afterwards. We'll hardly scratch the surface, but that's about all we'll have time for. It takes many days to sink your teeth into all the history."

"We've never been there," said Candice. "It sounds marvelous, and I hope I am speaking for everyone here when I say how much we really appreciate all your efforts. Not only your hard work which made all this come together, but your financial sacrifice as well."

With that, the group gave Scott a round of applause.

"Thank you so much. You all have had a big part in this."

"I looked at the website for the cherry blossoms, and we are only going to miss the peak by less than a week, so it should still be pretty colorful," said Kathy.

"Definitely," said Scott. "Just to wrap things up, I secured three suites, they will all be adjacent, and we can mingle until it is time to turn in. Speaking of that, we should all get a good night's sleep tonight, we have a couple of big days ahead of us."

CHAPTER 25

THE DISTRICT OF COLUMBIA

Mid-morning Thursday, the elongated plain white van pulled up into the Yamaguchi's driveway.

"No rain for the next few days," said the driver.

"Sixty in D.C.," said Scott. "I don't care if anyone has their underwear packed. As long as Mark has his paddles, I'm good."

"You're in rare form," said Kate.

The nine team members finished piling in the van and awaited the arrival of the Metro at the Hawthorne platform. The main rush had diminished, but a few men in suit coats boarded, along with a handful already seated. The group pondered who might be looking out for them. Without incident, the train rolled into Grand Central and the team began their trek to Penn Station.

"It's going to be a bit of a challenge to stay together, so let's stay in groups of three and gather near corners. As long as we have one Yamaguchi in each group, we'll get to the station. I say we go west to Broadway, and then head south."

"A little bit crazy, and certainly stimulating," exclaimed Carl, as the group headed south on Broadway.

"It's a stark comparison to your part of the country," said Leah.

"I think I'd rather fight a Muskie for a half hour than these cars."

"Like my dad would say, you have to appreciate the struggle."

A couple Amtrak officials directed them all to the same car when it was boarding time. Mostly business travelers occupied the train, and security seemed to be just a minor precaution. Outside of Union Station in D.C., a courtesy bus from the Mandarin Oriental Hotel waited for the team. As they boarded, Scott leaned over to the driver.

"Can you swing us past the Mead Center so we can get a look at it while things are normal around there? In two days it's going to be crazy, and there will be no time to take things in."

"No problem."

"Just a slow cruise past it is fine," said Scott.

The sweeping contoured glass of the center faced the waterfront and reflected the afternoon sun.

"Very impressive," said Koji. A little step up from our basement."

After the cruise along the waterfront, the van pulled up in front of the Mandarin Oriental.

"This lobby is incredible Scott. I don't know what I did to deserve this," said Carl.

"You and Candice gave Mark the opportunity to pursue his dreams."

"Your three suites are ready and waiting Mr. Kobara," said the person behind the desk.

"Carl," said Scott. "You guys take the family suite, since there are four of you. Skip, Leon, and I will take the middle, and that leaves the Yamaguchi's on the right."

"This place is amazing!" Said Kathy, walking towards one of the west facing windows. "The view. Look at the sea of cherry blossoms surrounding the Tidal Basin. There's the Jefferson Memorial. Wow!"

"Very inspiring" said Candice.

Here's a group text from Scott.

I know Mark especially will be the happy about this, and chef Koji as well. We have a 6:30 reservation downstairs in the Muze restaurant, so check out the menu.

Koji happily discarded his chef's hat, but still advised Mark to steer away from some items, and to keep the portions down. Mark obliged, as a reasonably sized steak accompanied his baked potato and peas. The mood was light, and the quasi-celebration dinner wrapped up.

At nine a.m. Friday morning, two limos pulled up in front of the hotel, and the entire party was whisked off to the White House. As planned, the session was a quick courtesy meet and greet photo op with the President in the blue room. The party had seconds to shake hands and share a few words with the Commander in Chief. Mark was instructed to be the last in line, so the President could spend a little extra time with him at the end. It was over in a snap, with little chance to bask in the aura of the moment. A staff member helped with the group photo, and the gathering was shuttled over to the United States Capitol for an intern led tour. At the conclusion of the visit, an official addressed the gathering.

"Thank all of you for visiting. The Linderman family, and Scott, you stay here with us. We'll take the rest of you to a DC Circulator stop, and you can hop on and off at your whim. The family should be finished about 2:30, and we will transport them to hook up with you, wherever you are at the time."

Back in a limo, the five guests were zipped off to the White House for the ceremony and luncheon. A string quartet played softly in the corner of the East Room as they entered.

"Look at all this elegance," said Kathy. "And I am invited because I slipped a teen onto a cruise ship."

"Shhh." whispered Scott. "I'm sure there have been other visitors to this room who have done a lot worse, myself excluded of course."

"It's a good thing we spruced up our wardrobe," said Candice, as one of the White House Social Aides glided over to intercept them.

"I'm Navy Lieutenant Commander Long, and I am here to help you feel at home. It can be a bit overwhelming, I know."

Officer Long and the five visitors intertwined their way through the dignitaries; The Chinese Ambassador, Consulate Generals. National Team Chief Coach and members. Effortlessly he introduced and mingled the parties using his knowledge of the Chinese language. The aide carried most of the workload effortlessly, and Scott pitched in as he acquainted his party with his fellow committee members. He stepped over to Mr. Ling, before introducing him.

The pair looked each other in the eye. Their handshake was firm and lengthy, as if cement their secret written agreement. Finally, Mark and his family caught up to Kai Meng. He was a young looking twenty four, wiry, with a build similar to Leon.

"This is Kai Meng."

In Chinese, Officer Long continued. "This is Mark Linderman, his mom, dad, aunt, and Scott, his team leader."

The opponents looked each other in the eye, shook hands, and smiled. A call to be seated came from up front. With all the guests settled at the ornate parallel tables, the President and the First Lady were announced. The attendees rose and delivered a resounding applause before taking their seats again. The President stepped up to a small podium flanked on his left by a female interpreter.

"Ladies and Gentleman, Ambassadors, Consuls, Committee Members, and team members of The United States and China, we welcome you. The reason we are here today, is because the leaders of these two great nations had a vision, fifty years ago when I was merely six years old. They had this idea of using the wonderful sport of table tennis as a vehicle to establish a relationship. And this relationship has flourished over the last fifty years. Today we come to commemorate that initial vision, and the accomplishments stemming from it. Tomorrow the celebration will culminate in a friendly competition, reminiscent of the original one. Now, please enjoy the delightful meal, compliments of the White House Staff."

"Maine Lobster, Gulf Shrimp, Angus Beef. Would Koji approve of this?" asked Scott jokingly.

As the luncheon wound down and the dishes were cleared, the head of the Diplomacy Committee took the podium.

"If we could have Kai and Mark up to the front."

Each player picked up a wrapped package from a small table off to the side and stood side by side.

"To commemorate the original exchange of gifts between Zhuang Zedong and Glen Cowan, Kai and Mark are going to exchange with each other some representative craftsmanship from each of their respective countries."

In succession, each player presented their gift with both hands. Kai opened his box and displayed the pens to the guests. Mark revealed a handmade silk kite, bearing the head of a dragon. A big round of applause followed, the two players shook hands, and an official took to the podium.

"That wraps it up for today. Thank you all for attending. We will see you tomorrow, and good luck gentlemen."

Where are you guys? texted Scott to Skip.

We're at the Lincoln Memorial, at the base of the stairs going up. We'll be over shortly.

In minutes the limo dropped off Mark's family and Scott.

"How was it?" asked Kate enthusiastically.

"The food was awesome," said Mark with a smile.

"It was very nice and relaxed. Not tense at all," said Candice.

"How was Kai?" asked Koji.

"Leon's size. He seemed friendly." said Scott.

"What did you guys do while we were gone?" asked Candice.

"We got hung up in the Smithsonian Museum of American History for quite a while, and then hit a few monuments," said Kate. "Why don't you guys go up and take in the view of the Reflecting Pool, and then we can hop back on the Circulator."

"I'll make a dinner reservation at the hotel," said Scott, moving away from the others, as he now sat high on the stairs. He looked around, and quickly called Jeff.

"This is the last time we will likely talk before tomorrow. Is everything set?"

"Yes. I did a test run this morning and took things to the brink of breaching their system without tipping them off. The temperature outside is ideal. If we were to have an unusual hot spell and the air conditioning was on, it would be a lengthier transition. But with the temperature around sixty, it's not going to take a lot to kick that temperature up inside, kind of like a simmering pot."

"Just remember," said Scott. "The games can greatly vary in length, but figure about seven minutes. Keep that in mind for the time it will take to warm things up. So if Mark is down say three games to one, you need to get busy."

"I hope you are right about all this."

"Don't worry about a thing. We'll talk afterwards."

"Yep."

Descending down the stairs of Honest Abe's Memorial, Scott's dishonest plot was finalized. The Chinese had been accused of hacking. Scott was having an American system hacked into in his attempt to defeat the Chinese. A Chinese product was being used to strike back at them as well—in the form of Leon Zeng. It was game on, behind the scenes.

The two parents and eight students from Hawthorne arrived, and met the team downstairs in the Muze. Koji governed Mark's eating for the very last time. Most likely, the students would want to stay up late and do a little suite hopping, but Mark needed to stay away from those distractions. Today was a full day, and a huge day awaited.

Two years ago, this was unimaginable. Mark had met Leah, seen new parts of the country, and trained with champions. A team was behind him. He developed social skills, gained popularity, and was off to an Ivy League school. He had met the president, and soon would be in focus on worldwide television. A new world was ahead of him, regardless of the outcome tomorrow.

By contrast, Scott could not stop and smell the cherry blossoms. The behind the scene machinations held him hostage. His lifelong goal, reputation, and possibly freedom were on the line. An opportunity like this would never again arise in his lifetime. Victory was imperative.

CHAPTER 26

THE THEATER OF OPERATION

The first ball was scheduled to be put into play at 1:00 p.m., but Scott and company were asked to arrive at 11:00 a.m. The group piled into the shuttle and were shortly detained at a checkpoint near the arena. Officers walking German Shepherds were visible, but the sharpshooters likely lurking on rooftops were not. Men in dark suits strolled around the perimeter, entrance, and interior of the facility. The team was led through a rear door and shown where Mark could change and prepare before the match.

"Let me give you a bird-s eye view of the stage," said the hostess. "Actually it's not high at all. There's not a bad seat in the house."

Upstairs, they emerged onto the carpeted corridor behind the last row of seats. The perfectly centered blue table contrasted with the reddish temporary floor, focalizing viewer's attention. A technician moved a light meter around the table to verify the level of illumination. Television cameras were optimally positioned at multiple locations. An overhead cam hung from the infrastructure above the table. Technical crews finalized their preparations.

"Your seats are the third row ones over there on the north side. Koji, you have the end seat which gives you easy access to coach Mark, if you two need to consult between games. The group from Hawthorne High will be sitting directly behind you. On the south side across from you in the front row, will be the Chinese dignitaries and ambassadors. Oh, and by the way, the front row seats below you will be occupied by the President, and his family. Seated in the row behind them, and off to the sides will be secret service agents."

"Whoa," said Skip.

"Mark, you can change into your warmups because you and Koji have an interview that will be pre-recorded. The rest of you can check out the facility. There is a lounge with refreshments where you can hang out until we start seating."

Leon sported a crew cut, and a tad more facial hair. Transitional glasses obscured his eyes. His appearance was nothing like his playing days.

"Leon," said Scott. I arranged for you to trade seats with someone higher up in a different section. The Chinese will likely be paying attention to who is seated in our group."

Mark changed and joined Koji. With the table in the background, an ABC cameraperson and a sports commentator walked up to the pair. After a brief introduction, a microphone was held in front of Koji, and the bright lights came on.

"We're talking with United States top player Mark Linderman and his coach Koji Yamaguchi. Koji came close to upsetting the top Chinese player in the world in 1997. Koji, besides the technological changes in the balls and the paddles, what has changed as far as style of play since then?"

"Today's player is more aggressive. Passive chopping and blocking are quickly taken advantage of. One must be an all-around attacker."

"Mark's background was exclusively playing against robots. How were you able to help transition him to playing against live competition?"

"I didn't have to do much. He has always been a student of the game, and is able to adapt his style quickly to whatever is thrown at him."

"Mark, how has Koji helped you?"

"Koji is innovative. He uses unusual props and different mental approaches."

"How has this rise to the top changed your life?"

"I have met many great people. My supporters have all been wonderful."

"Thanks guys."

Koji and Mark were led to a large meeting room where they were greeted by the familiar sound of ping pong balls being struck. Two temporary tables occupied the middle, roughly fifteen feet apart. The committee felt that separate rooms would not be in the spirit of diplomacy. At the far table, Kai and his coach casually exchanged shots while engaging in light conversation. They stopped their rallying, and the four nodded to acknowledge each other. Mark remained in his warmups, did some stretching, and eased into his warmup routine with Koji. As the appearance on the big stage grew closer, the players stepped up their intensity. The sounds reverberating from the hard surfaced room, began to reflect the acute strikes, and the short intervals between them.

With such tight security, the select crowd filtered in much slower than for a normal production. One by one, the padded mauve seats absorbed the patrons, who were devoid of heavy outerwear. Scott and the five others moved into their row. Two parents and eight students from Hawthorne filed in, settling in behind them. In the catwalk above, one agent overlooked each of the four seating sections.

Except for the first two rows in the North and South sections, the theater was full. The Chinese diplomats, ambassadors, and delegation, were led in from a floor level entrance, accompanied by a security detail. The crowd greeted them with a courteous standing ovation, and round of applause. As they quieted, double doors opened from the opposite side of the theater, President Blansfeld, the First Lady, along with their teen son and daughter, walked to their seats. A lengthy and rousing round of applause greeted them as well.

The intimate setting was already warm in the social sense. Relations between the United States and China had improved dramatically since President Blansfeld took office merely three months ago. Tariffs were falling off products like spent blossoms on cherry trees, and the President's approval rating ramped upwards. The diplomatic ball was already in motion, and the coincidental timing of Ping Pong Diplomacy II was set to metaphorically add more positive spin.

The secret service agents sat down after the president, their tiny earpieces just visible to the Lindermans, directly behind them. Eight bubbly Hawthorne teens added to the pre-match buzz now encompassing the theater. The agents took the reasonable level of disorder behind them in stride. The President wanted to be seated directly in the mix of the families, hoping to enhance his already approachable image. So where better to place him than in the midst of Mark's parents and supporters. Not even a toothpick was getting inside, and the only malice that could penetrate the building was looming—in the form of bits and bytes. A sterling performance by Mark would suppress that, and the countdown was on.

Two officials walked into the arena and took their spots behind their scorer's tables, opposite each other, in line with the net. Traditional flip over scorecards sat on each table, which augmented the temporary electronic scoreboard hanging above.

Following the officials in, were the two players side by side in their warm-up gear, each carrying sports totes. The emcee, dressed in a dark suit, and holding a wireless microphone, walked in behind them.

"Ladies and gentlemen, we are gathered at this historic event to celebrate a lasting friendship between the People's Republic of China and the United States of America. Fifty years ago, the table was set. Two countries separated by thousands of miles of ocean, became separated by nine feet, and competed on a level playing surface. Goods and services began to flow between the two countries as fluently as the ping pong balls that started the relationship. That relationship has continued to expand. Now, two players will engage in a friendly competition on this metaphoric table, to launch us into another fifty years of cooperation."

A huge round of applause erupted, and the emcee continued.

"Before I begin the introductions, there are some things I must mention. All cell phones must be off, and you must not take them out. If you stand up from your seat during the match, your situation will be considered urgent, and you will be addressed by agents. The format of this event is the following. Each game is played to eleven points. If the game is tied at ten, the winner must win by two points. This is a six game out of eleven series. The first player to win six games, wins the match. The players will change sides every two games. I will begin the introductions of the players, and the national anthem of each country will follow. After the anthems, the players will engage in a five minute warm-up period. Please hold your applause until both players have been introduced."

"Representing The People's Republic of China, and beginning play at the east end of the arena is Kai Meng. Representing The United States of America, and beginning play at the west end of the arena is Mark Linderman."

A lengthy round of applause ensued, and *The March of the Volunteers* was followed by *The Star Spangled Banner*. Both players sat on padded folding chairs, opposite each other, in line with the net. With a signal from one of the officials, each removed their warmups, took a few sips of water, and walked over to their respective sides. By agreed upon protocol, both player's outfits were absent of any logos or advertising. Kai's shorts and collared shirt were both blue with white stripes and accents. Mark sported black shorts and a collared black shirt as well, with yellow stripes diagonally interspersed.

Inside the gymnasium at Hawthorne High, students populated the folding chairs covering the floor. Scott popped for a premium sixteen by nine foot screen, a super high definition projector, and an audio video receiver which piped the sound into the gym speakers. Supporters brought in dark sheets from home and blocked off the light which beamed through the upper windows.

"Mark's got a hot getup on," said Melanie to Hannah.

The officials walked over the table, and as is customary, inspected both paddles. There were no surprises, Tenergy and Mark V. One of the officials pulled a new plastic ball out of the box and handed it to Kai.

"Okay gentlemen, begin your five minute warmup."

Immediately, the forehand to forehand exchanges crisscrossed the net at a staggering pace, especially to the uninitiated onlookers. The sound of the sharply struck balls confirmed their velocity.

"The ratio of reflected sound to absorbed sound is perfect," said Scott, leaning over to Leah and Kate. "Crisp, like the plucked strings of a Stradivarius."

The waning minutes before the showdown gave Scott a small window to sit back and enjoy the beauty of the game. Backing out of this potential ploy was now tricky. There was no way to communicate with Jeff. His only way out was running down to a tournament official, and issuing an earth shattering mea culpa. But with all that was invested, that wasn't going to happen. The players completed their warm up, retreated to their respective chairs, and hydrated. After one minute, the tournament official gave the word, and it was game on.

CHAPTER 27

THE HEAT IS ON

There was no bigger stage than this one, at least in the table tennis world. Kai came in with the edge when it came to major tournament experience, and Mark would touch the hottest stove so far in his young playing career. Eclipsing the predicted highs, the bright early afternoon sun pushed the outside temperature into the mid-sixties. Combining that with the packed theater, and additional camera lighting, a touch of cool air needed to be introduced into the Fichandler.

Both players crouched at the opposite ends of the table. Kai, stared at the ball in his open left palm, and lofted it three feet into the air. His backhand sidespin serve jumped off Mark's paddle perfectly to his forehand side where Kai smashed it for the winner. Mark consistently practiced neutralizing this setup with Leon, but executing under these real conditions was a different ballgame. It was an ominous start, but Mark always needed some kind of wake up call. Koji sat unfazed as usual, for now. A couple of jaw dropping rallies loosened up both players and energized the crowd. The initial butterflies had escaped, and the high speed chess match was in full swing. Mark fought back with a very respectable performance, but lost game one 11-8. Mark enjoyed a short-lived one point lead in the middle of game two, but again came up short 11-9.

Grace and finesse by both players interspersed the *rock-em sock-em* power game. Like Mark, Kai possessed variety and adaptability, and was executing a tad better to win the game of millimeters so far. The players switched playing ends, and in the biggest nail biter so far, Mark squeaked out a 14-12 win in game three. He now trailed two games to one, and the collective anxiety of Mark's supporters ticked slightly downwards.

Training with the best had closed the gap between Mark and the best Chinese players. On the other side of the arena, the Chinese support team appeared as if it was just another day at the office. Americans rarely gave them problems at the highest level of play. Game four would be a pivotal one, they would be tied, or Mark would trail 3-1. Although imperceptible to many, the fourth game was a bit sloppier than the prior three, with unforced errors on both sides. Kai benefited from an early edge clipper, and never looked back to win 11-7.

Back in his family room, Jeff's fingers were frozen from the fear of involving himself. At the match, Scott squirmed in his seat, gazing in all directions as if to visibly detect puffs of warm air. With Mark trailing 7-4 in the fifth game, Jeff paced back and forth with his laptop nearly morphing into sleep mode. He took another look at his television, and broke out of his funk. With a deep breath, he aligned the mouse pointer on the send button, and clicked. He placed his face into the palms of his hands as the cyber-thermal attack began. At the speed of light, the electrical impulses raced through the invisible boundaries of the nation's capital, and breached the Fichandler.

No one inside the theater was going to hear any evidence of air ducts expanding, but the first to recognize a temperature change would be the people in the top seats, and the secret service agents on the catwalk. Mark succumbed in that fifth game, again 11-8. Now down four games to one, Mark was in serious trouble. Koji was not allowed to go down and coach him until the break after game six.

The airborne attack infused the theater with its first onslaught of warm air. Mark managed to sneak out to an early 3-1 lead in game six before any subtle change began to infiltrate the arena floor. Now, temporarily, Willis Carrier's invention was locally offline, and Mark's hypersensitive skin began to sense the absence of the coolness it produced.

The nature of rising warm air necessitated an extra boost to deliver the balmier conditions to the floor level. The spectators who came in with light removable outerwear wiggled and struggled in their seats to purge themselves of these garments. This shuffling and general sense of restlessness, now injected a tinge of background noise into the previously quiescent conditions.

Mark's body and soul not only got the restorative effects from the warmth, but the slight rustling in the seats eased the tension as well. He subconsciously felt more at home, and confident. In quick fashion he eased to an 11-6 victory in game six. The Chinese were not concerned, Mark was due to win one, and Kai just threw him a diplomatic bone. As the players sat down for their break, Jeff immediately cut the heat, giving the initial blast time to meld with the existing air. If he baked the cake too fast, everything would come to a halt. Amazed that his actions could influence play, Jeff again reactivated the system as the players returned to action with Mark now down four games to two.

As game seven was underway, an arena official holding his two-way radio exited out a pair of double doors with a tournament official trailing close behind him. The Chinese just wanted the match to be finished, figuring it was a done deal. They could endure the uncomfortable conditions for the remainder of the contest. Secret Service agents on the catwalk, held their radios to their ears. Back in the center of the Fichandler, Mark was thriving and delivered a solid 11-7 win in game seven.

The Chinese had been slow to react, but concern was rapidly mounting. Heads turned from side to side, as they whispered in each other's ears. When Mark bolted ahead 7-4 in game eight, a light bulb went off. The correlation between the temperature and the score flashed like mars lights above a squad car. When Mark went to retrieve an errant shot, committee member Ling abruptly rose from his seat and instantly three Chinese officials followed suit. Mark now led 8-4.

The Chinese coach called over to the now sweat covered Kai, and told him to request a timeout to stop play. The coach waved at the head tournament official, who was waiting to hear back from the facility engineer. Four Chinese officials walked over the head official and joined in a group huddle. The remaining Ping Pong Diplomacy II committee members walked onto the floor, and a rejuvenated Scott joined the mix. The discussion became increasingly animated, and before it erupted into a public and high profile shouting match, officials herded the group out through the double doors and into the hallway. Jeff temporarily neutralized the onslaught of heat.

After ten minutes, the groups returned to their seats and the head tournament official took the floor and addressed the crowd.

"Ladies and gentlemen, we apologize for the unexpected spike in the temperature we are all experiencing. The facility engineers are working on the problem. Because of the distance our guests have travelled, we do not want to have to have this historic event end in such a fashion. It is not logistically possible to continue this tomorrow, so we have reached an agreement. The end of game eight will be played in the current conditions. If Mr. Linderman wins, the match will be tied 4-4. If Mr. Meng wins, he will go ahead 5-3. The engineers estimate that it will take thirty minutes to shut down and reboot the entire facility. If they are successful in restoring the temperature to normal, the match will be played to its entirety. If they are not successful, the results will stand the way they are after game eight. The players will now have a three minute warmup, and game eight will resume.

With that, Jeff poured in a short final blast of heat before his screen reverted back to the login page. After several frantic attempts, he concluded he was locked out of the system, and was now helpless to intervene. Kai and Mark returned to the table. Mark served, and proceeded to take the next two points. After Kai picked up the first point of his serve, Mark pulverized his patented backhand smash for an outright winner. The match was now tied at four games each, and the tournament official again addressed the crowd.

"We have thirty minutes. You can stand up and stretch, and make a restroom visit if you need to. Players and coaches can proceed to the staging room to keep their player warmed up."

CHAPTER 28

THE EXCLAMATION POINT

Mark's team members jockeyed for position around Scott, and Skip was the first to ask the foremost question.

"What went on in those discussions?"

"Initially, they wanted the last two games to be voided. Then they were going to settle for replaying the last game in normal conditions. I pounded the table that both players were subject to the same environment, so just keep playing. I knew that wouldn't fly, but they did compromise. I guess they wanted to appear diplomatic on the national stage."

"Okay Scott, give us the real dirt," said Skip.

"I pointed out that this event is not a sanctioned tournament, where exact environmental conditions are specified. I did guarantee the lighting would be brought up to tournament specifications, but didn't say anything about temperature. When the Chinese committee members visited this place, they were so impressed, that they must have just assumed that comfortable conditions were a given. So anyway they threatened to walk out. But in the national spotlight, no way they were going to do that. We'll certainly hear about it later."

The emcee returned to the stage floor.

"The preliminary report I just received from the engineers, is that they expect the system to be up and stabilized within the thirty minute time agreement." Applause erupted from the now stirring crowd.

Before Koji was set to head back with Mark into the warmup room, he signaled over to Leon and the three huddled, talking strategy. With Scott engaged in animated conversation with one of the Chinese committee members, Mark and Leon slipped down to the double doors, and Mark addressed the tournament official.

"Koji sent his assistant down to warm me up, if that's okay. He said the heat was getting to him a bit."

"Sure. No problem. Does Koji need medical attention?"

"No. He just didn't want to exert himself."

Scott caught a glimpse of the pair just as they were disappearing into the hallway. Abruptly ending his conversation and chasing them down would have put attention right where he didn't need it. He eased out of the dialog and stormed back to the seats to confront Koji.

"What are you doing sending him in there?"

"The balmy conditions are affecting me. He's warming Mark up. He'll be fine."

With Leon donning Dockers and a polo shirt, Kai and his coach did a double take when he walked in, but immediately got back to business. Leon deliberately took his position at the north end of the table like Kai's coach. He tempered his play as to not give any hints of his style. When he bent down to pick up a ball underneath the table, he quickly reached down the front of his shirt and pulled out a leather necklace. He oriented his back to the coach as he exchanged forehands with Mark. The now dangling pendant, swung wildly from side to side.

When Kai's coach went to the corner of the room to retrieve a missed shot, Leon stopped his play, and the hanging pendant came to a rest. Leon waved his paddle at Kai, and with his left hand pointed at the red oversized *Z*, and trailing lightning bolt. Kai locked his eyes onto Leon's trademark. With disbelief, he glanced upwards to confirm that he was looking at his ex-teammate, and the ex-champion of the world. Leon hastily tucked this manifestation of his identity back under his shirt. Kai continued to catch quick glimpses of Leon each time the ball fell out of play.

The tournament official stepped into the practice room and signaled to the group that play was getting ready to resume. Leon and Kai's coach returned to their seats while the players waited behind the double doors with the official who turned on his microphone.

"Ladies and Gentlemen. The temperature as you can certainly feel is normal, and actually a touch cool. But it is stabilized and should soon come up to a comfortable level. The players will have a five minute warmup before completing the remaining two out of three games."

Mark and Kai went over to their respective chairs, grabbed some water, and cleaned the surfaces of their paddles. The audience now settled back quietly in their seats.

At the Hawthorne gymnasium, the students remounted their enthusiasm. *ABC Sports*, caught off guard by the delay in the match, now returned live, after switching to pregame baseball coverage. The players again walked over to the table and began their warmup.

Leon's surprise appearance seemed to distract Kai, especially since he witnessed Leon's carefree demeanor. It was obvious Leon wasn't there under duress, he was having fun with his reveal. It was a rebel move of epic proportions, one that Kai would relish if he only knew the details. Although Kai's face took on a look of bewilderment, he pounded the balls back to Mark. He could do a warmup routine in his sleep.

The players returned to their seats for a one minute freshening up, and finally stepped up to the table. Scott was back to wringing and intertwining his hands. He was unaware that the Zengmaster had flaunted his presence. Now, each competitor was outside his comfort zone. Mark was physically cool, and Kai was mentally distracted. Two experts would attempt to mentally overcome these outside elements. Scott's control of the physical side was gone, Mark's psychological ploy was now present. He played his wild card—face up to Kai, but invisible to the world.

Both players were slightly off their game as they begin play. Back and forth they exchanged points, with Mark maintaining the edge, 4-3, 7-6, and then 10-9. In an epic point, where the players intoxicated the crowd with transitions from offense to defense and back, Mark capped off the game with a colossal forehand game winner. The jubilant crowd did its best to remain seated, loudly expressing its collective pleasure.

The mind has little room for outside thoughts during a high level table tennis match, and it appeared by his glances into the seats, that Leon was hanging around upstairs in Kai's attic. Mark and Kai changed ends, taking a little extra time to collect themselves. Mark served, and after six volleys, fast blocked Kai's slam for an outright winner. The next point, he reached into his auxiliary toolkit for a demoralizing gem. Setting the table with some close to the net pushes, he delivered a no-look misdirected backhand flick. The severely angled and stealthily executed shot caught the far right stripe on Kai's side, spinning out of reach. The crowd exploded with appreciation witnessing a rarely executed shot in the era of power table tennis.

Exchanging points is all Mark needed to do, but playing cautious is dangerous, and not what elevates players to the top. So

Mark, holding the mental edge augmented by his last surprise point, returned to his mixed attack. He stretched his lead to 7-4, and maintained it to match point 10-7.

The forty-five square foot table in the center of the Fichandler Theater is dwarfed by the twenty- thousand square foot ice rink at the Herb Brooks Arena in Lake Placid. But forty-one years later, on this smaller and dissimilar surface, a single point would unleash another miracle. One cough pierced through the otherwise inaudible crowd, preceding Mark's unfettered pre-serve routine. In the control booth, the needle on the audiometer was firmly pegged to the left. Scott, the support team, Jeff, and the students back home, sat in nervous anticipation.

Mark lobbed the ball upwards from his open left palm, and his serve just skirted over the net. Kai, who normally would chop back the serve elected to aggressively flip the offering. In a split second, Mark took the ball at its apex, and pulverized the plastic projectile with his patented backhand blast. The exclamation point sent the Fichandler crowd to their feet with a robust round of applause. In much more chaotic fashion, The Hawthorne High School auditorium erupted into a frenzy. In respect for his opponent, Mark quelled his celebratory urge, and nodded to Kai. The players walked over to each other and shook hands as the emcee took to the floor.

"Ladies and gentlemen, let's have another round of applause for the extraordinary display of talent we have witnessed this afternoon. The tournament director will present participation plaques to both players, and the President of the International Table Tennis Federation will present the winning trophy to Mark"

With secret service agents, maneuvering around the perimeter of the floor, President Blansfeld and his family walked over to shake hands of the two participants, and then proceeded over to the Chinese delegation. No one would dare set forth on the floor, so Mark rambled up to the seats, and one by one exchanged hugs with his team, along with the Hawthorne teens and parents. Once Mark completed an abbreviated interview, the team began to file out. Koji pulled Leon aside.

"Mark told me you would be able to tip off Kai without the coach picking up on it. How did you pull that off?"

Kai slyly poked the necklace above the v-line of his shirt.

"Where did you get that? And how did you get it through security?"

"Mark had the leather strap, and together we went over to the basement of the library where they have the *makerspace*. We drew up the design, and we produced the pendant on the 3-D printer—plastic."

"A page out of my book. Brilliant!"

At that point Scott walked over and the subject immediately changed.

"We need to shuffle out of here. Leon, there's going to be an *Uber* for you that will take you separately back to the hotel just to be safe.

"By the way. Did Kai recognize you in the warmup room?" asked Scott.

"I don't think he paid much attention to me," said Leon, glancing over at Koji and smiling.

As Kai sat in the darkened cabin of the Boeing 777, he pulled the small wooden box set from his carry-on bag. He removed the cherry wood pen, and began gliding it over an envelope on his tray. His even strokes immediately produced smooth black circles. Kai returned it and grabbed the writing instrument encased in the aromatic pine. He scratched and scrawled, only to produce clear indentations. It appeared the cartridge was bad—strange that a high profile gift wouldn't have been tested. Kai turned the top of the pen counterclockwise, and unscrewed it from the barrel. Protruding upwards was a tightly scrolled piece of paper, sitting in place of the cartridge. He extracted the hidden stationery, and worked it along the edge of his tray to straighten it.

The message was short, and contained an e-mail address at the end. *Leon here. If you won, I am happy for you. If you lost, I hope you are not scorned. If you ever want a place to stay, or a pendant with your name on it——.*

THE END

Acknowledgements

I would like to thank my playing buddies for their support, especially the guys at Sunset Knoll. One of them, Al, a fellow competitor and world cruiser, may have planted the seed for this. I would like to thank writing coach Renee Nicholls at mywritingcoach.net for her valuable feedback during the developmental phase. Thanks to the technical staff at the Elmhurst Public Library for their occasional assistance. Also, kudos to Will Shortz for unknowingly sparking a couple ideas for this story. A shout out to Nicholas Griffin for his wonderful book, Ping-Pong Diplomacy: The Secret History Behind the Game That Changed the World. And to Fred Danner's work, Adventures of the Ping Pong Diplomats.

About the Author

In the early stages of pursuing this work, Ken Robbins discovered the very short list of table tennis fiction on the shelves, or in cyberspace. Tips on technique and strategy were readily available in various forms of media, and rightfully so. Most players want to improve their game, the author included. So, hoping his pen is mightier than his paddle, or maybe his keystrokes have more impact his forehand slam, Ken seeks to fill some of this fictional void in *The Ping of the Seas*.

Ken lives and plays in the west suburbs of Chicago.

Read more at www.krobbinz.com and www.twitter/@binzthinkin